A LUCKY LUKE ADVENTURE

MA DALTON

BY MORRIS & GOSCINNY

Original title: Lucky Luke – Ma Dalton
Original edition: © Dargaud Editeur Paris 1971 by Goscinny and Morris
© Lucky Comics
www.lucky-luke.com
Translator: Frederick W Nolan
Lettering and text layout: Imadjinn sarl
This edition published in Great Britain in 2007 by
Cinebook Ltd
56 Beech Avenue
Canterbury, Kent
CT4 7TA
www.cinebook.com
Fourth printing: December 2017
Printed in Spain by EGEDSA
A CIP catalogue record for this book
is available from the British Library
ISBN 978-1-905460-18-2

9th CINEBOOK
The 9th Art Publisher

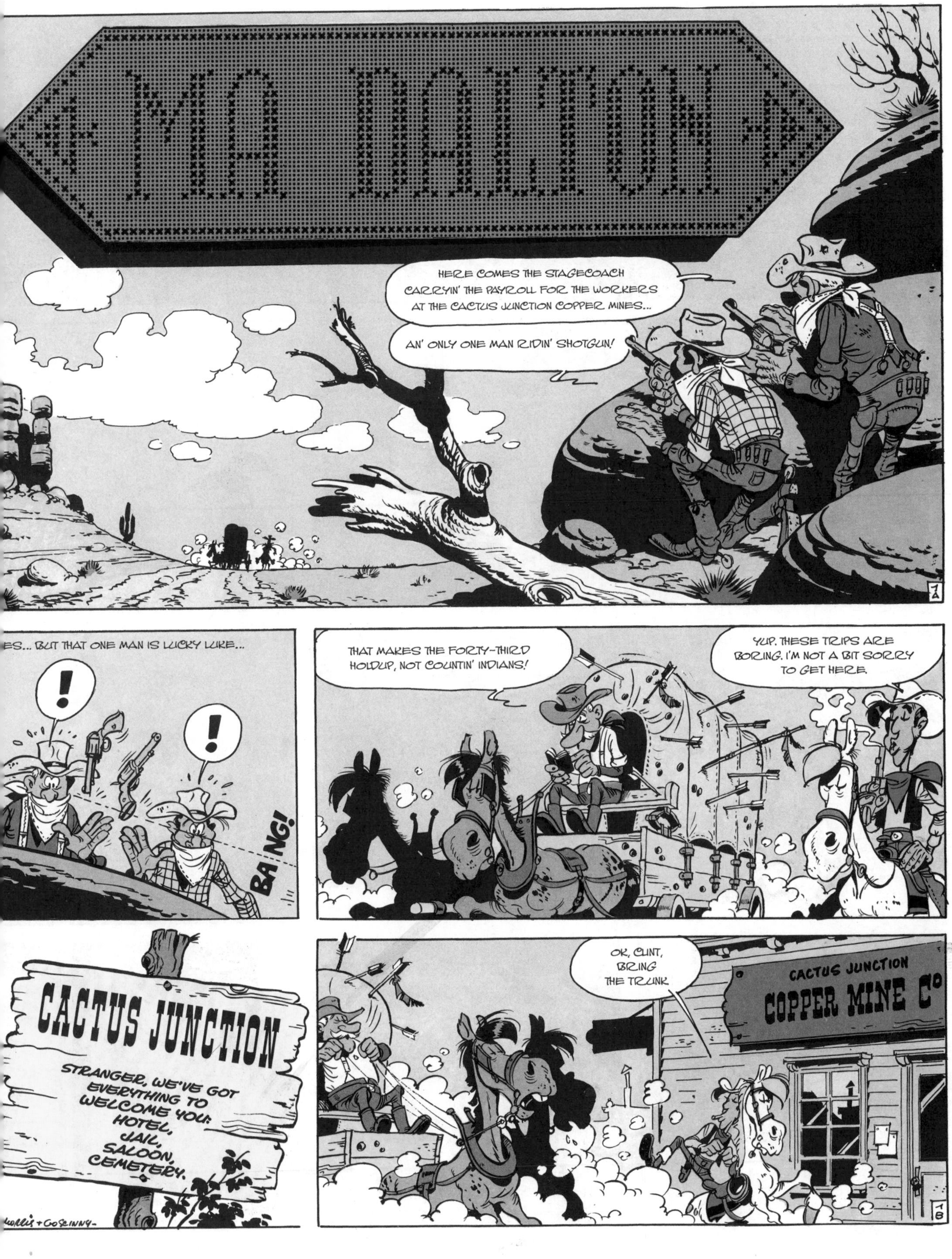

MA DALTON
HERE COMES THE STAGECOACH CARRYIN' THE PAYROLL FOR THE WORKERS AT THE CACTUS JUNCTION COPPER MINES...
AN' ONLY ONE MAN RIDIN' SHOTGUN!
ES... BUT THAT ONE MAN IS LUCKY LUKE...
!
!
BANG!
THAT MAKES THE FORTY-THIRD HOLDUP, NOT COUNTIN' INDIANS!
YUP. THESE TRIPS ARE BORING. I'M NOT A BIT SORRY TO GET HERE.
CACTUS JUNCTION
STRANGER, WE'VE GOT EVERYTHING TO WELCOME YOU: HOTEL, JAIL, SALOON, CEMETERY.
Morris + Goscinny
OK, CLINT, BRING THE TRUNK
CACTUS JUNCTION
COPPER MINE Co

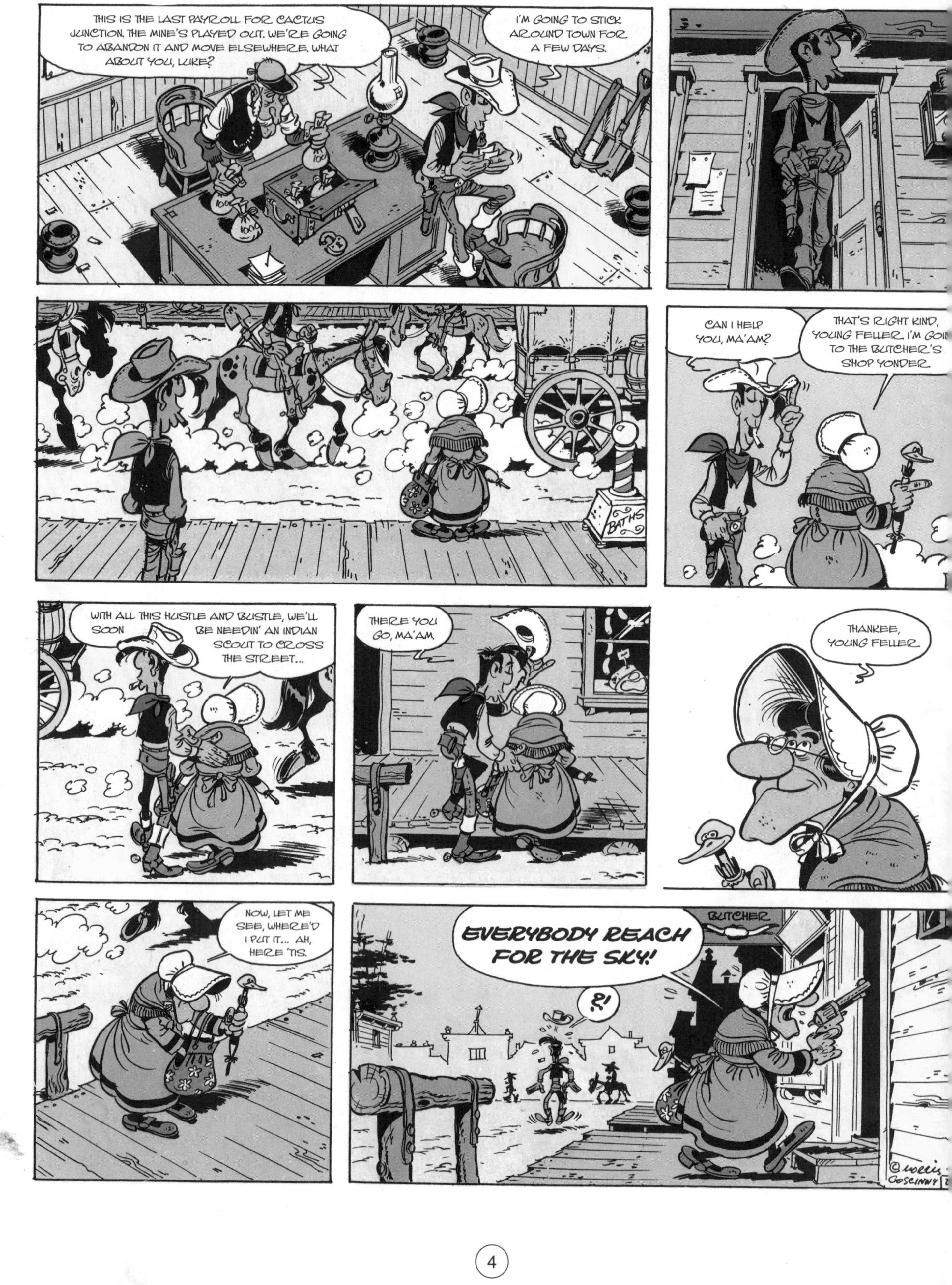

THIS IS THE LAST PAYROLL FOR CACTUS JUNCTION. THE MINE'S PLAYED OUT. WE'RE GOING TO ABANDON IT AND MOVE ELSEWHERE. WHAT ABOUT YOU, LUKE?
I'M GOING TO STICK AROUND TOWN FOR A FEW DAYS.
BATHS
CAN I HELP YOU, MA'AM?
THAT'S RIGHT KIND, YOUNG FELLER. I'M GOIN TO THE BUTCHER'S SHOP YONDER.
WITH ALL THIS HUSTLE AND BUSTLE, WE'LL SOON BE NEEDIN' AN INDIAN SCOUT TO CROSS THE STREET...
THERE YOU GO, MA'AM
THANKEE, YOUNG FELLER.
NOW, LET ME SEE, WHERE'D I PUT IT... AH, HERE 'TIS.
BUTCHER
EVERYBODY REACH FOR THE SKY!
?!
© MORRIS GOSCINNY

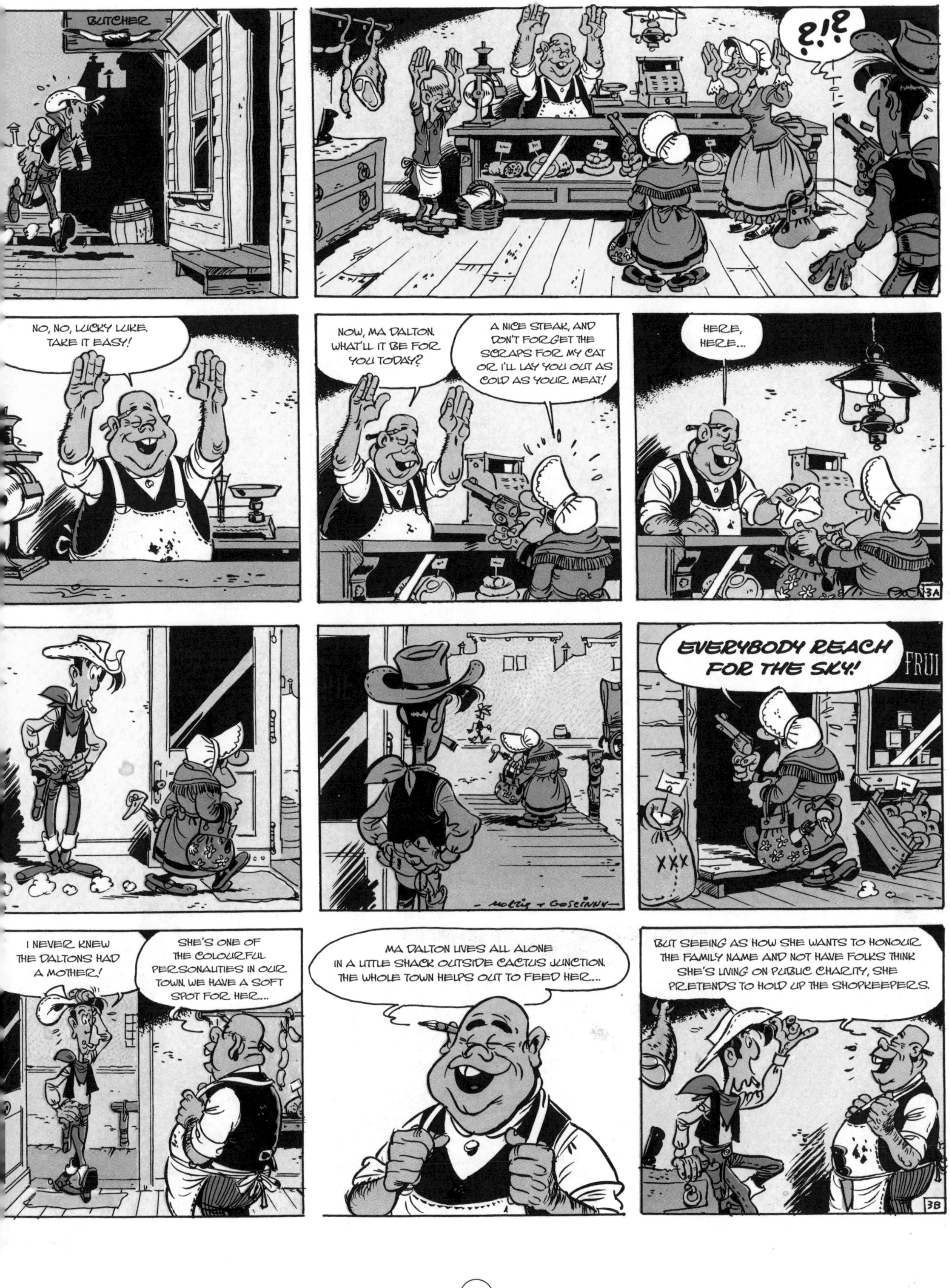
BUTCHER
?!?
NO, NO, LUCKY LUKE. TAKE IT EASY!
NOW, MA DALTON. WHAT'LL IT BE FOR YOU TODAY?
A NICE STEAK, AND DON'T FORGET THE SCRAPS FOR MY CAT OR I'LL LAY YOU OUT AS COLD AS YOUR MEAT!
HERE, HERE...
3A
EVERYBODY REACH FOR THE SKY!
FRUI
XXX
MORRIS + GOSCINNY
I NEVER KNEW THE DALTONS HAD A MOTHER!
SHE'S ONE OF THE COLOURFUL PERSONALITIES IN OUR TOWN. WE HAVE A SOFT SPOT FOR HER...
MA DALTON LIVES ALL ALONE IN A LITTLE SHACK OUTSIDE CACTUS JUNCTION. THE WHOLE TOWN HELPS OUT TO FEED HER...
BUT SEEING AS HOW SHE WANTS TO HONOUR THE FAMILY NAME AND NOT HAVE FOLKS THINK SHE'S LIVING ON PUBLIC CHARITY, SHE PRETENDS TO HOLD UP THE SHOPKEEPERS.
3B

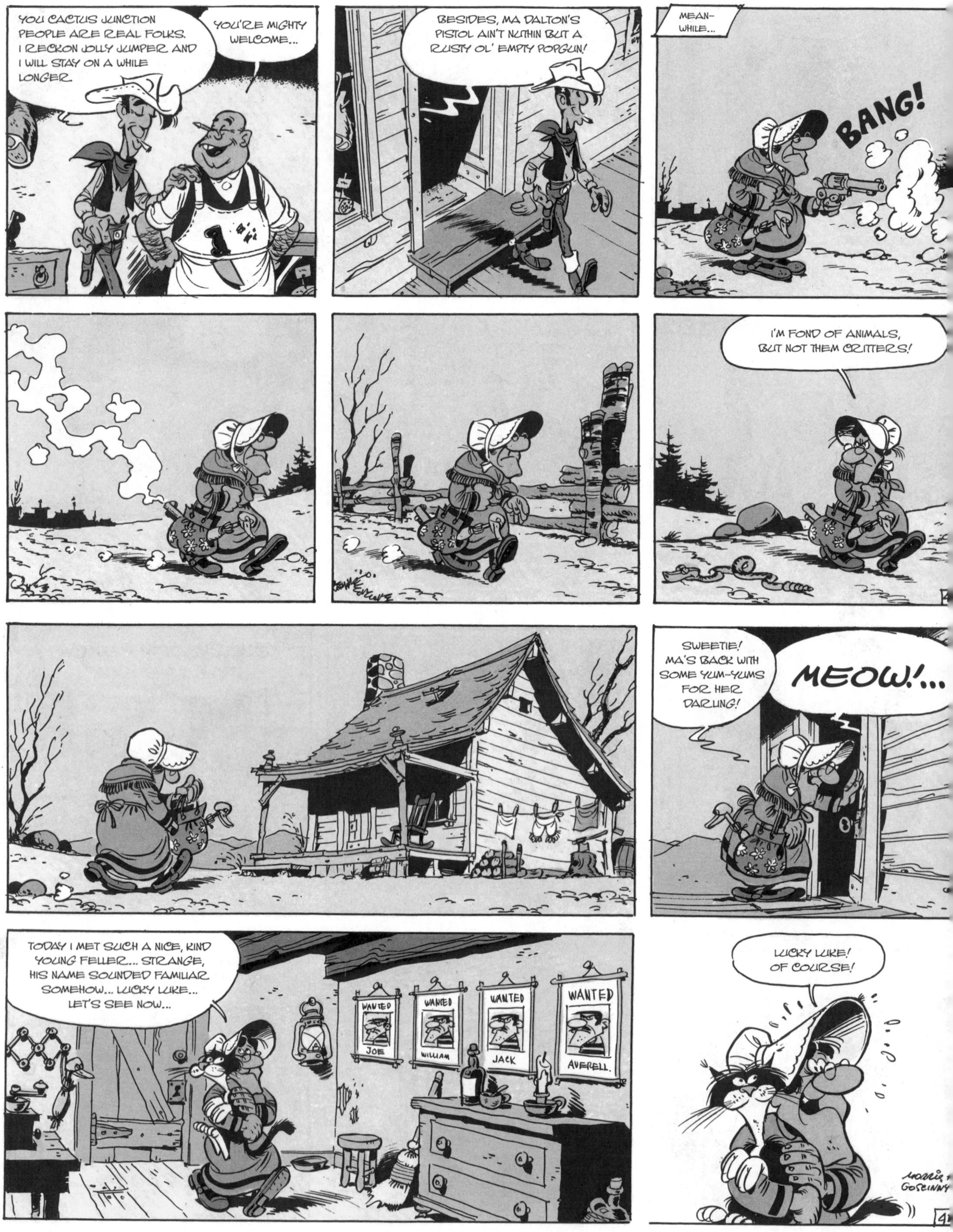

YOU CACTUS JUNCTION PEOPLE ARE REAL FOLKS. I RECKON JOLLY JUMPER AND I WILL STAY ON A WHILE LONGER.
YOU'RE MIGHTY WELCOME...
BESIDES, MA DALTON'S PISTOL AIN'T NUTHIN BUT A RUSTY OL' EMPTY POPGUN!
MEAN-WHILE...
BANG!
I'M FOND OF ANIMALS, BUT NOT THEM CRITTERS!
SWEETIE! MA'S BACK WITH SOME YUM-YUMS FOR HER DARLING!
MEOW!...
TODAY I MET SUCH A NICE, KIND YOUNG FELLER... STRANGE, HIS NAME SOUNDED FAMILIAR SOMEHOW... LUCKY LUKE... LET'S SEE NOW...
WANTED
JOE
WANTED
WILLIAM
WANTED
JACK
WANTED
AVERELL.
LUCKY LUKE! OF COURSE!
MORRIS GOSCINNY

LUCKY LUKE, YOU KNOW, SWEETIE? HE'S THE ONE KEEPS PUTTIN' MAH BOYS IN PRISON!*

*SEE DALTON CITY

FUNNY, AIN'T IT? RECKON I OUGHT TO WRITE AND TELL THE BOYS!

COURSE, IF THEY'VE ESCAPED, THEY WON'T GET THE LETTER... I'LL PUT "PLEASE FORWARD" ON THE ENVELOPE...

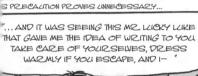

THIS PRECAUTION PROVES UNNECESSARY...

"...AND IT WAS SEEING THIS MR. LUCKY LUKE THAT GAVE ME THE IDEA OF WRITING TO YOU TAKE CARE OF YOURSELVES, DRESS WARMLY IF YOU ESCAPE, AND I—"

WHAT'S THIS HERE LETTER?

IT'S A "G."

...AND I GIVE YOU ALL A GIG GEAR HUG. AND AVERELL, MY GAGY...

ENOUGH!

LUCKY LUKE! I DON'T WANT HIM TO GET AWAY! LET'S GET OUT OF HERE! RIGHT NOW!

TAKE IT EASY, JOE!

YEAH, JOE, TAKE IT EASY!

OW WE GONNA DO IT, JOE? IT TAKES TIME TO DIG A TUNNEL.

YEAH! 'SPECIALLY SINCE THEY'VE PUT US ON THE THIRD FLOOR...

WE'RE GONNA BURN DOWN THE PRISON!

BUT WHERE'LL WE GO WHEN THEY CATCH US AGAIN?

GIT UP, GAGY!

MORRIS + GOSCINNY

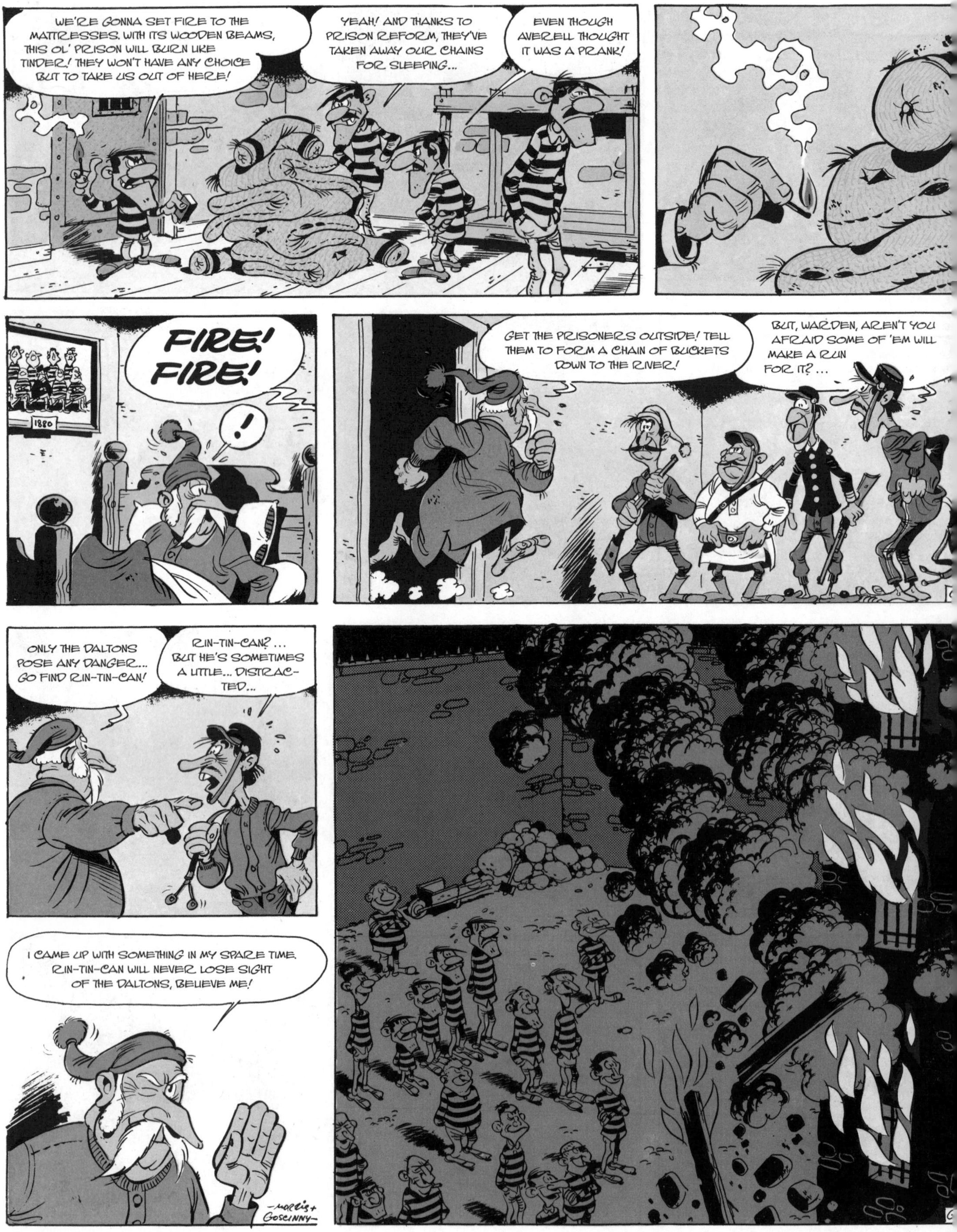
WE'RE GONNA SET FIRE TO THE MATTRESSES. WITH ITS WOODEN BEAMS, THIS OL' PRISON WILL BURN LIKE TINDER! THEY WON'T HAVE ANY CHOICE BUT TO TAKE US OUT OF HERE!
YEAH! AND THANKS TO PRISON REFORM, THEY'VE TAKEN AWAY OUR CHAINS FOR SLEEPING...
EVEN THOUGH AVERELL THOUGHT IT WAS A PRANK!
1880
FIRE! FIRE!
!
GET THE PRISONERS OUTSIDE! TELL THEM TO FORM A CHAIN OF BUCKETS DOWN TO THE RIVER!
BUT, WARDEN, AREN'T YOU AFRAID SOME OF 'EM WILL MAKE A RUN FOR IT? ...
ONLY THE DALTONS POSE ANY DANGER... GO FIND RIN-TIN-CAN!
RIN-TIN-CAN? ... BUT HE'S SOMETIMES A LITTLE... DISTRACTED...
I CAME UP WITH SOMETHING IN MY SPARE TIME. RIN-TIN-CAN WILL NEVER LOSE SIGHT OF THE DALTONS, BELIEVE ME!
MORRIS + GOSCINNY

WE'RE GOING TO GIVE YOU BUCKETS AND YOU WILL FORM A FIRE-FIGHTING CHAIN... JOE DALTON, COME HERE!

?

GIVE ME YOUR WRIST, JOE.

ONLY A GOOD FILE WOULD WORK ON THIS LEASH, JOE, AND THAT WOULD TAKE TIME. RIN-TIN-CAN WILL NEVER TAKE HIS EYES OFF OF YOU

CLIC!

IF HE TRIES TO ESCAPE, BITE HIM, EH, RIN-TIN-CAN!

SO HE'S MY NEW MASTER?

PROVIDED HE'S GOOD TO ME... I'M READY TO SHOWER HIM WITH AFFECTION AND PLEDGES OF DEVOTION...

7A

WARDEN!! THE WATER BUCKETS HAVE STOPPED COMING! THERE MUST HAVE BEEN AN ESCAPE!...

IN FACT...

7B

9

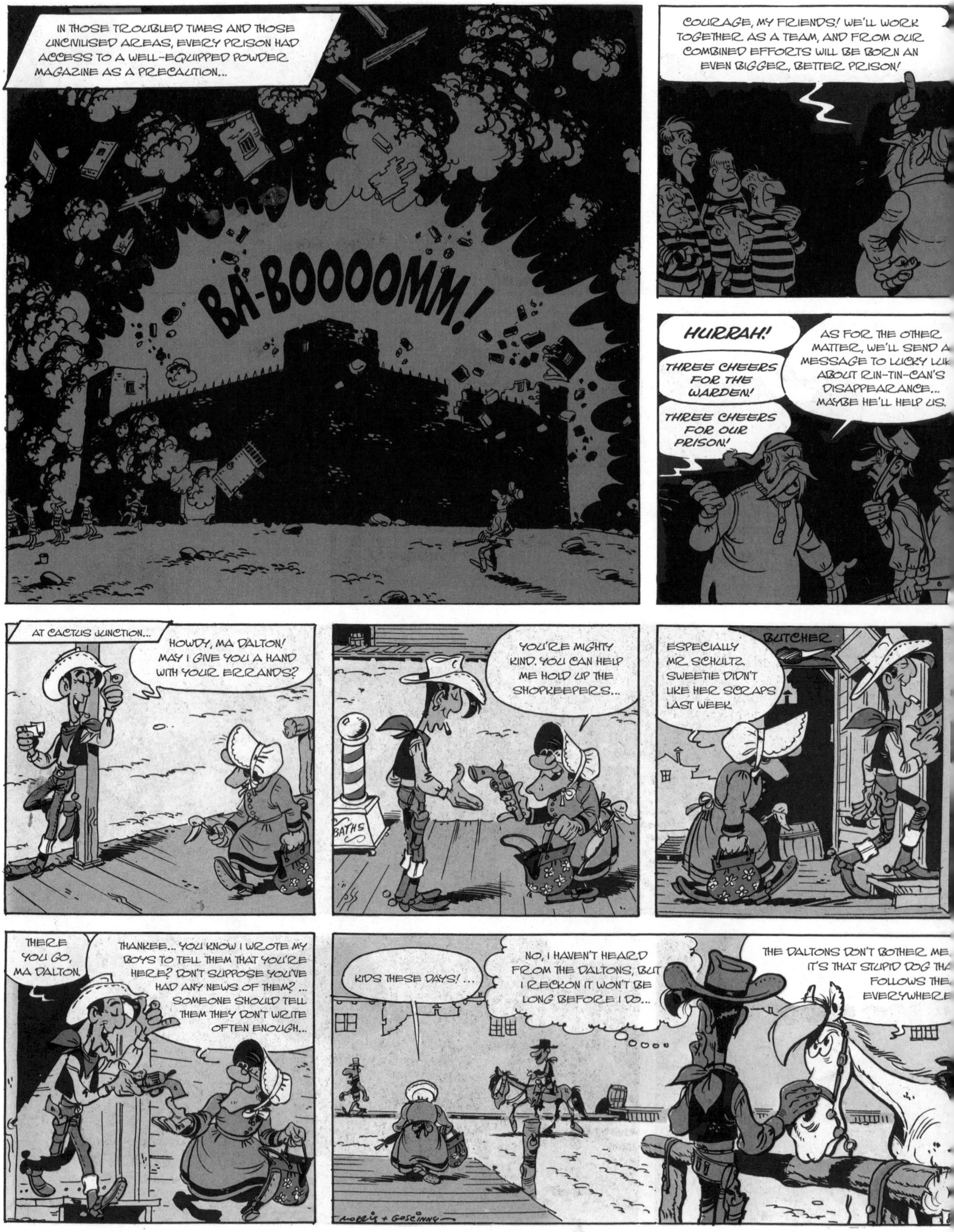

IN THOSE TROUBLED TIMES AND THOSE UNCIVILISED AREAS, EVERY PRISON HAD ACCESS TO A WELL-EQUIPPED POWDER MAGAZINE AS A PRECAUTION...
BA-BOOOOMM!
COURAGE, MY FRIENDS! WE'LL WORK TOGETHER AS A TEAM, AND FROM OUR COMBINED EFFORTS WILL BE BORN AN EVEN BIGGER, BETTER PRISON!
HURRAH!
THREE CHEERS FOR THE WARDEN!
THREE CHEERS FOR OUR PRISON!
AS FOR THE OTHER MATTER, WE'LL SEND A MESSAGE TO LUCKY LUK ABOUT RIN-TIN-CAN'S DISAPPEARANCE... MAYBE HE'LL HELP US.
AT CACTUS JUNCTION...
HOWDY, MA DALTON! MAY I GIVE YOU A HAND WITH YOUR ERRANDS?
YOU'RE MIGHTY KIND. YOU CAN HELP ME HOLD UP THE SHOPKEEPERS...
BATHS
BUTCHER
ESPECIALLY MR. SCHULTZ. SWEETIE DIDN'T LIKE HER SCRAPS LAST WEEK.
THERE YOU GO, MA DALTON.
THANKEE... YOU KNOW I WROTE MY BOYS TO TELL THEM THAT YOU'RE HERE? DON'T SUPPOSE YOU'VE HAD ANY NEWS OF THEM? ... SOMEONE SHOULD TELL THEM THEY DON'T WRITE OFTEN ENOUGH...
KIDS THESE DAYS! ...
NO, I HAVEN'T HEARD FROM THE DALTONS, BUT I RECKON IT WON'T BE LONG BEFORE I DO...
THE DALTONS DON'T BOTHER ME. IT'S THAT STUPID DOG THA FOLLOWS THE EVERYWHERE
MORRIS + GOSCINNY

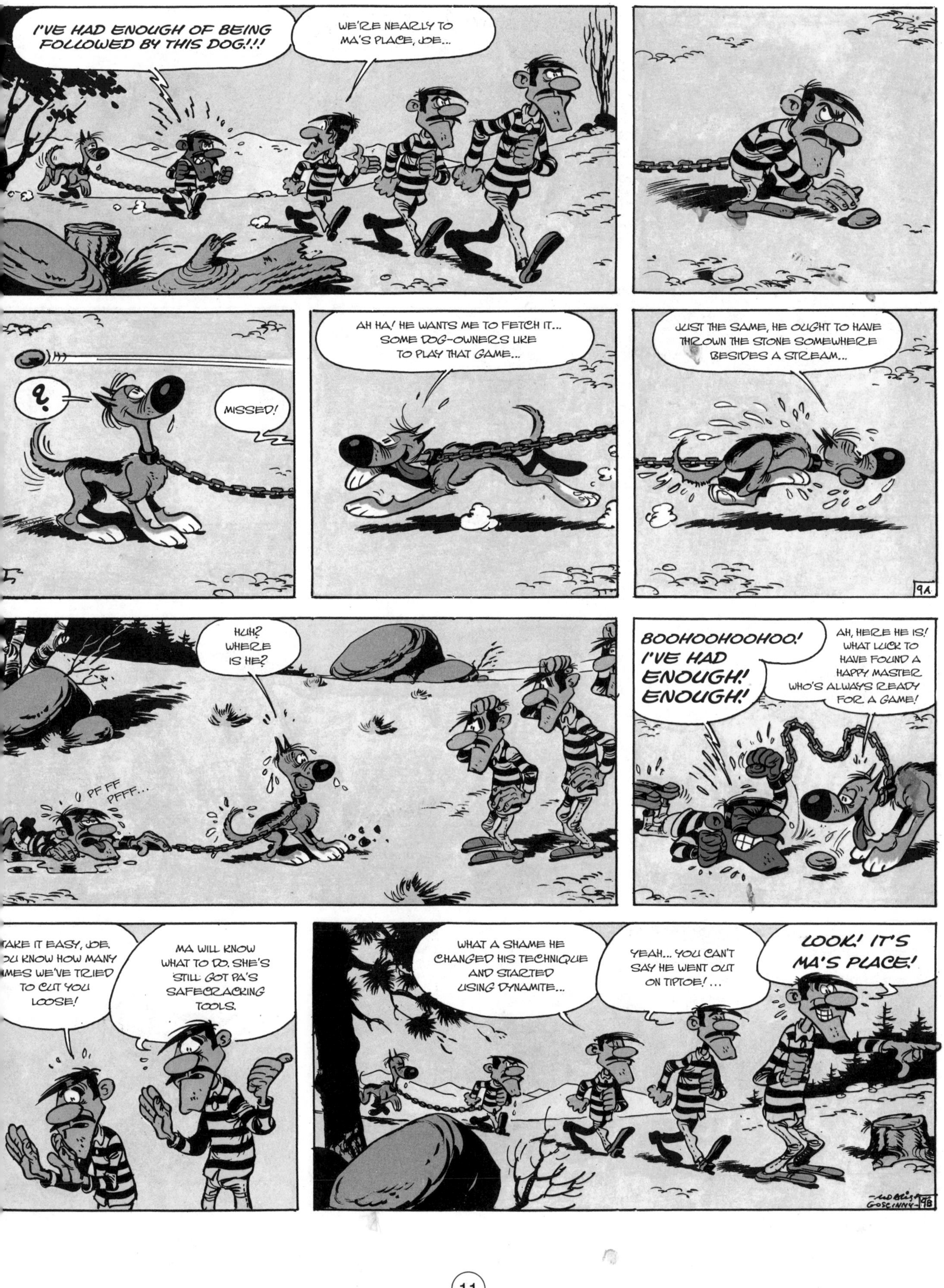
I'VE HAD ENOUGH OF BEING FOLLOWED BY THIS DOG!!!
WE'RE NEARLY TO MA'S PLACE, JOE...
?
MISSED!
AH HA! HE WANTS ME TO FETCH IT... SOME DOG-OWNERS LIKE TO PLAY THAT GAME...
JUST THE SAME, HE OUGHT TO HAVE THROWN THE STONE SOMEWHERE BESIDES A STREAM...
9A
HUH? WHERE IS HE?
PF FF PFFF...
BOOHOOHOOHOO! I'VE HAD ENOUGH! ENOUGH!
AH, HERE HE IS! WHAT LUCK TO HAVE FOUND A HAPPY MASTER WHO'S ALWAYS READY FOR A GAME!
TAKE IT EASY, JOE. OU KNOW HOW MANY IMES WE'VE TRIED TO CUT YOU LOOSE!
MA WILL KNOW WHAT TO DO. SHE'S STILL GOT PA'S SAFECRACKING TOOLS.
WHAT A SHAME HE CHANGED HIS TECHNIQUE AND STARTED USING DYNAMITE...
YEAH... YOU CAN'T SAY HE WENT OUT ON TIPTOE! ...
LOOK! IT'S MA'S PLACE!
9B

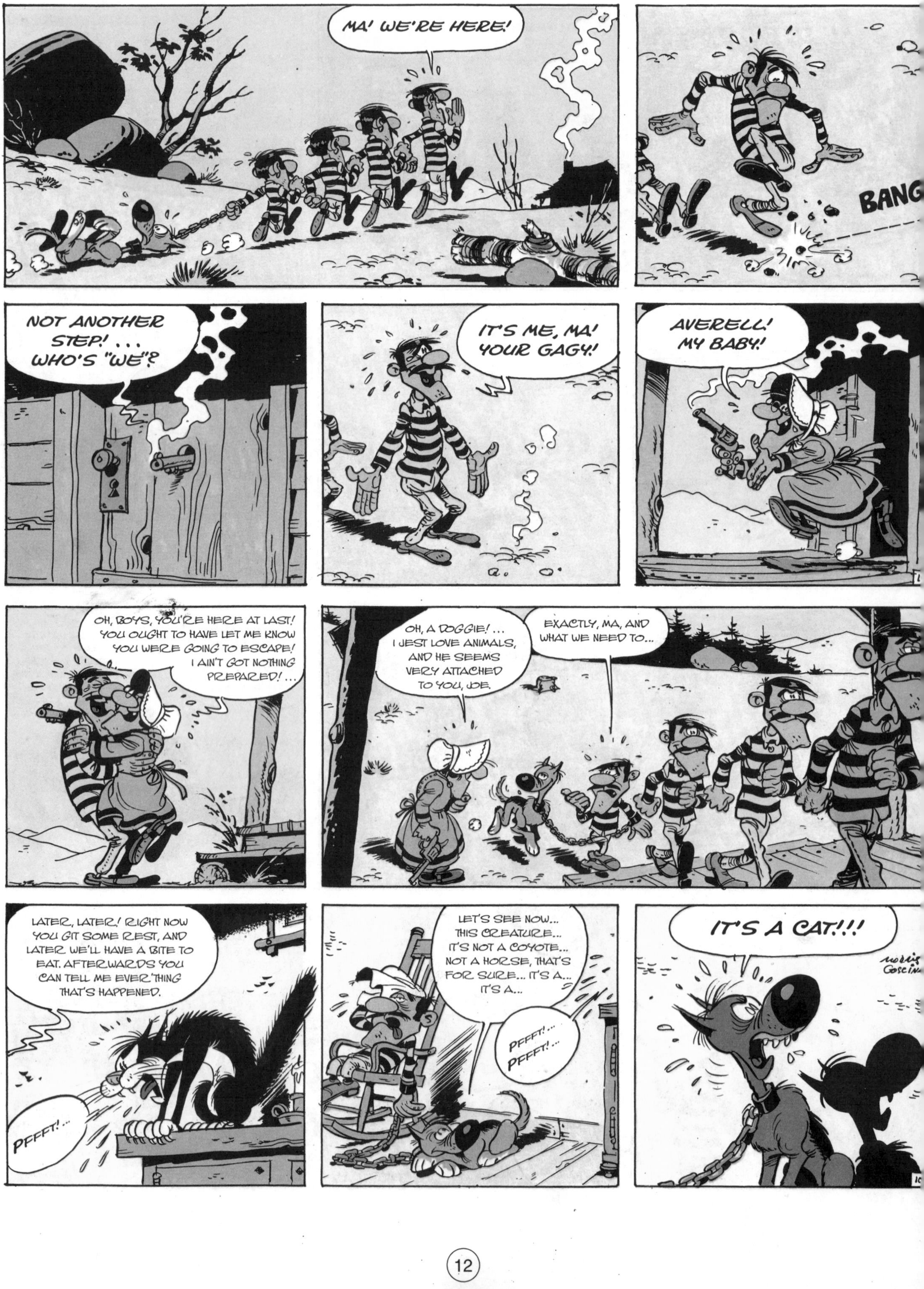
MA! WE'RE HERE!
BANG
NOT ANOTHER STEP! ... WHO'S "WE"?
IT'S ME, MA! YOUR GAGY!
AVERELL! MY BABY!
OH, BOYS, YOU'RE HERE AT LAST! YOU OUGHT TO HAVE LET ME KNOW YOU WERE GOING TO ESCAPE! I AIN'T GOT NOTHING PREPARED! ...
OH, A DOGGIE! ... I JEST LOVE ANIMALS, AND HE SEEMS VERY ATTACHED TO YOU, JOE.
EXACTLY, MA, AND WHAT WE NEED TO...
LATER, LATER! RIGHT NOW YOU GIT SOME REST, AND LATER WE'LL HAVE A BITE TO EAT. AFTERWARDS YOU CAN TELL ME EVER'THING THAT'S HAPPENED.
PFFFT! ...
LET'S SEE NOW... THIS CREATURE... IT'S NOT A COYOTE... NOT A HORSE, THAT'S FOR SURE... IT'S A... IT'S A...
PFFFT! ... PFFFT! ...
IT'S A CAT!!!

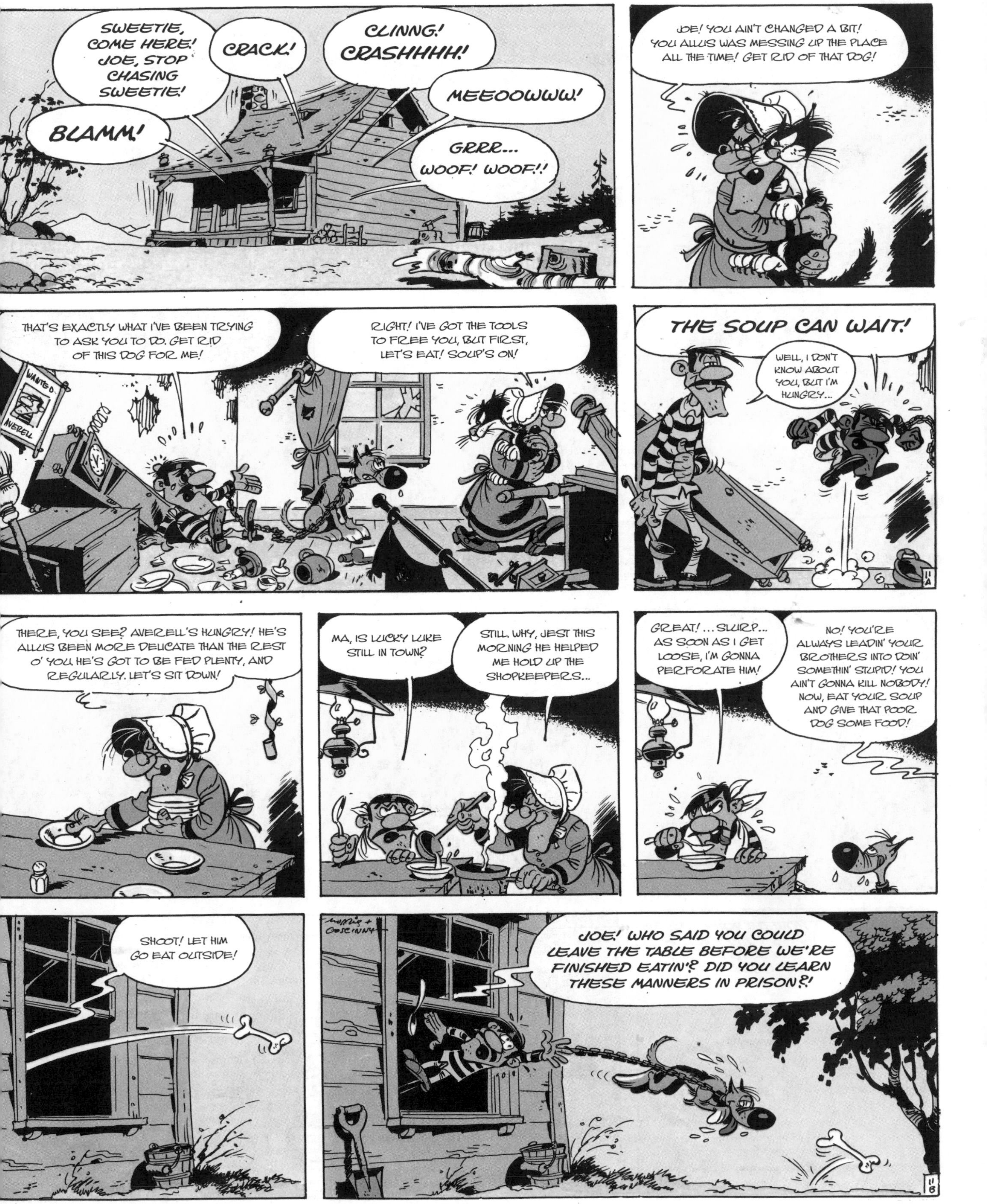
SWEETIE, COME HERE! JOE, STOP CHASING SWEETIE!
BLAMM!
CRACK!
CLINNG! CRASHHHH!
MEEOOWWW!
GRRR... WOOF! WOOF!!
JOE! YOU AIN'T CHANGED A BIT! YOU ALLUS WAS MESSING UP THE PLACE ALL THE TIME! GET RID OF THAT DOG!
THAT'S EXACTLY WHAT I'VE BEEN TRYING TO ASK YOU TO DO. GET RID OF THIS DOG FOR ME!
WANTED
AVERELL
RIGHT! I'VE GOT THE TOOLS TO FREE YOU, BUT FIRST, LET'S EAT! SOUP'S ON!
THE SOUP CAN WAIT!
WELL, I DON'T KNOW ABOUT YOU, BUT I'M HUNGRY...
THERE, YOU SEE? AVERELL'S HUNGRY! HE'S ALLUS BEEN MORE DELICATE THAN THE REST O' YOU. HE'S GOT TO BE FED PLENTY, AND REGULARLY. LET'S SIT DOWN!
MA, IS LUCKY LUKE STILL IN TOWN?
STILL. WHY, JEST THIS MORNING HE HELPED ME HOLD UP THE SHOPKEEPERS...
GREAT! ... SLURP... AS SOON AS I GET LOOSE, I'M GONNA PERFORATE HIM!
NO! YOU'RE ALWAYS LEADIN' YOUR BROTHERS INTO DOIN' SOMETHIN' STUPID! YOU AIN'T GONNA KILL NOBODY! NOW, EAT YOUR SOUP AND GIVE THAT POOR DOG SOME FOOD!
SHOOT! LET HIM GO EAT OUTSIDE!
MORRIS + GOSCINNY
JOE! WHO SAID YOU COULD LEAVE THE TABLE BEFORE WE'RE FINISHED EATIN'?! DID YOU LEARN THESE MANNERS IN PRISON?!

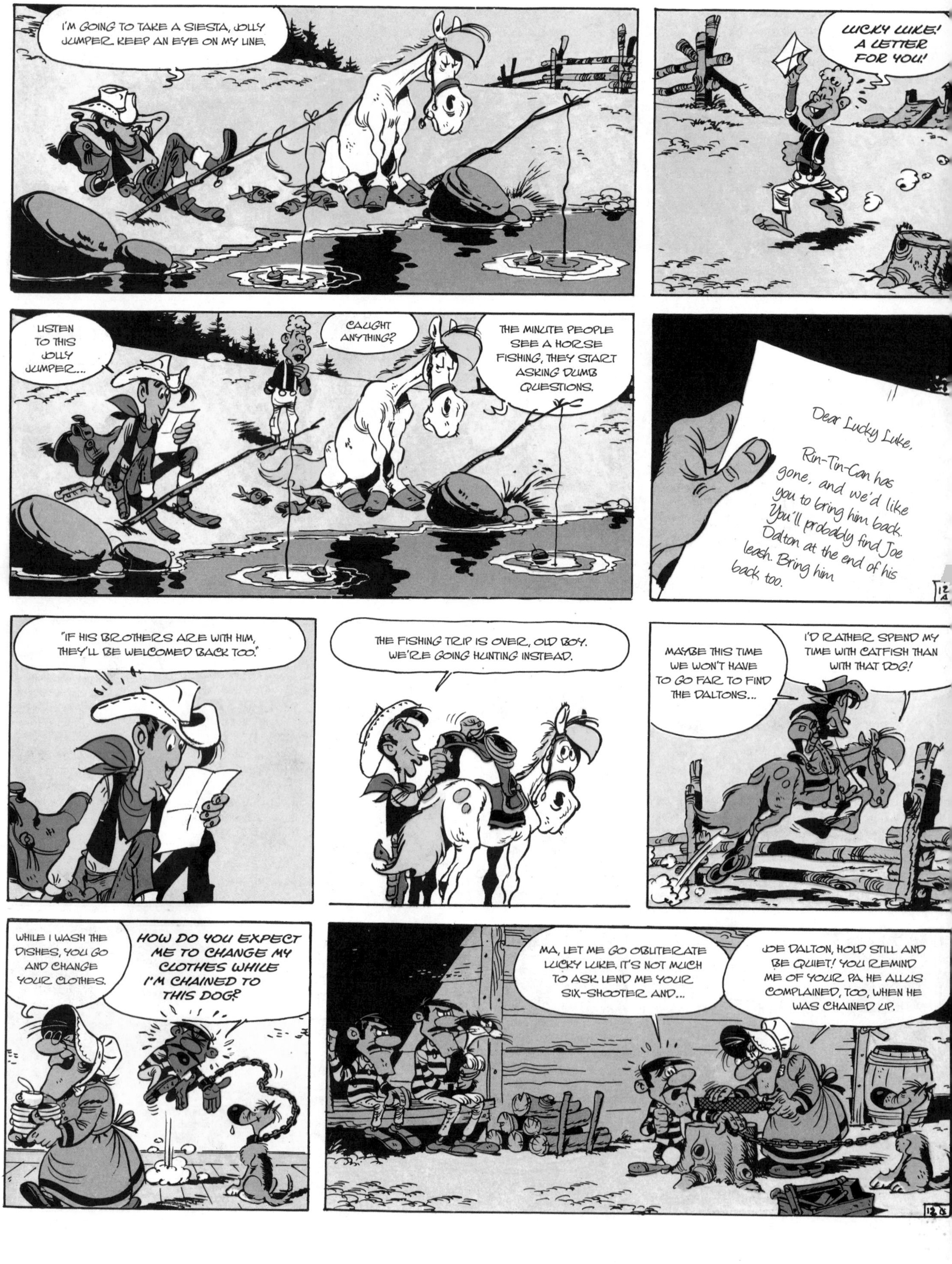
I'M GOING TO TAKE A SIESTA, JOLLY JUMPER. KEEP AN EYE ON MY LINE.
LUCKY LUKE! A LETTER FOR YOU!
LISTEN TO THIS JOLLY JUMPER...
CAUGHT ANYTHING?
THE MINUTE PEOPLE SEE A HORSE FISHING, THEY START ASKING DUMB QUESTIONS.
Dear Lucky Luke,
Rin-Tin-Can has gone, and we'd like you to bring him back. You'll probably find Joe Dalton at the end of his leash. Bring him back too.
"IF HIS BROTHERS ARE WITH HIM, THEY'LL BE WELCOMED BACK TOO."
THE FISHING TRIP IS OVER, OLD BOY. WE'RE GOING HUNTING INSTEAD.
MAYBE THIS TIME WE WON'T HAVE TO GO FAR TO FIND THE DALTONS...
I'D RATHER SPEND MY TIME WITH CATFISH THAN WITH THAT DOG!
WHILE I WASH THE DISHES, YOU GO AND CHANGE YOUR CLOTHES.
HOW DO YOU EXPECT ME TO CHANGE MY CLOTHES WHILE I'M CHAINED TO THIS DOG?
MA, LET ME GO OBLITERATE LUCKY LUKE. IT'S NOT MUCH TO ASK. LEND ME YOUR SIX-SHOOTER AND...
JOE DALTON, HOLD STILL AND BE QUIET! YOU REMIND ME OF YOUR PA. HE ALLUS COMPLAINED, TOO, WHEN HE WAS CHAINED UP.

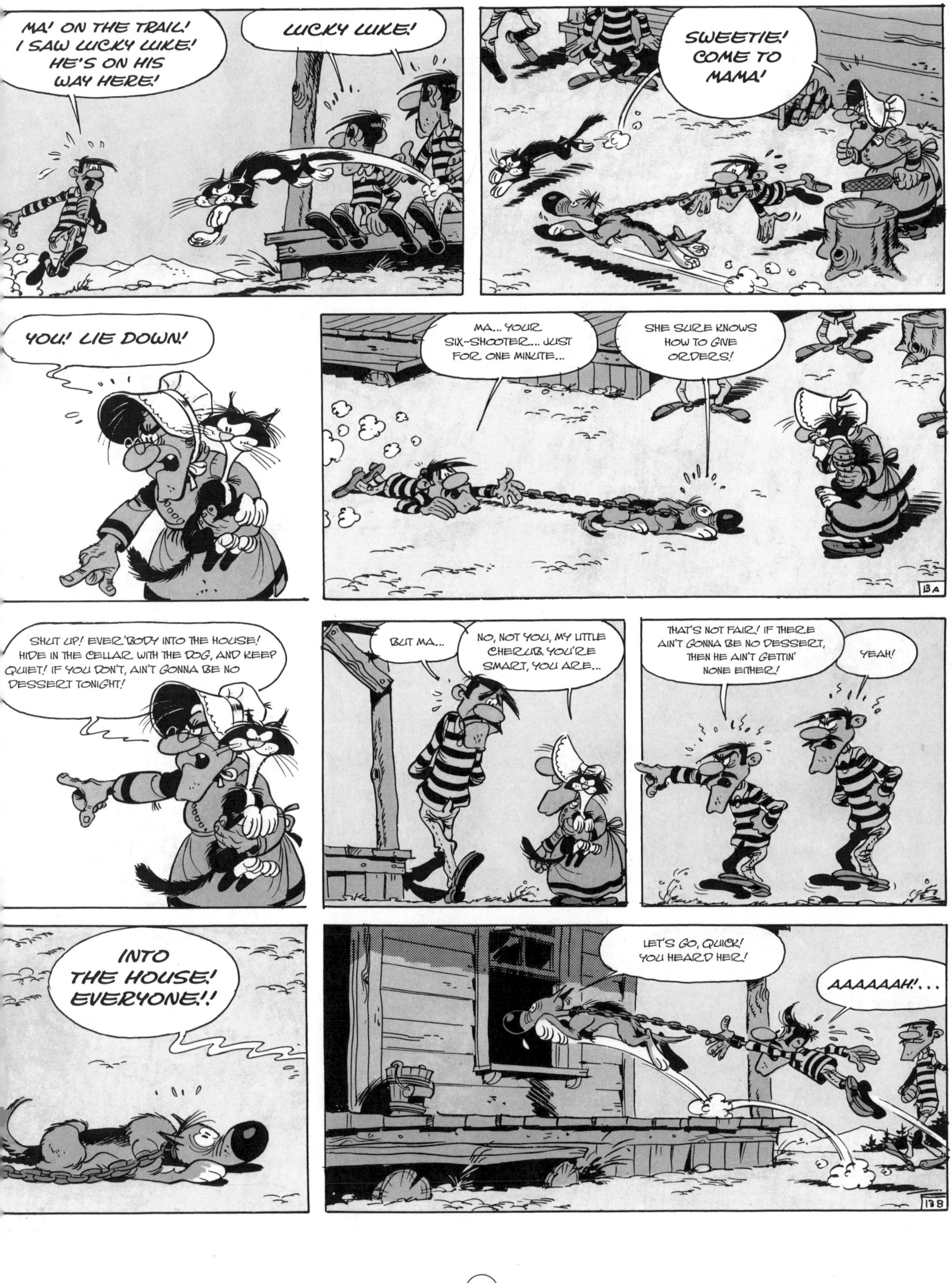

MA! ON THE TRAIL! I SAW LUCKY LUKE! HE'S ON HIS WAY HERE!
LUCKY LUKE!
SWEETIE! COME TO MAMA!
YOU! LIE DOWN!
MA... YOUR SIX-SHOOTER... JUST FOR ONE MINUTE...
SHE SURE KNOWS HOW TO GIVE ORDERS!
13A
SHUT UP! EVER'BODY INTO THE HOUSE! HIDE IN THE CELLAR WITH THE DOG, AND KEEP QUIET! IF YOU DON'T, AIN'T GONNA BE NO DESSERT TONIGHT!
BUT MA...
NO, NOT YOU, MY LITTLE CHERUB. YOU'RE SMART, YOU ARE...
THAT'S NOT FAIR! IF THERE AIN'T GONNA BE NO DESSERT, THEN HE AIN'T GETTIN' NONE EITHER!
YEAH!
INTO THE HOUSE! EVERYONE!!
LET'S GO, QUICK! YOU HEARD HER!
AAAAAAH!...
13B

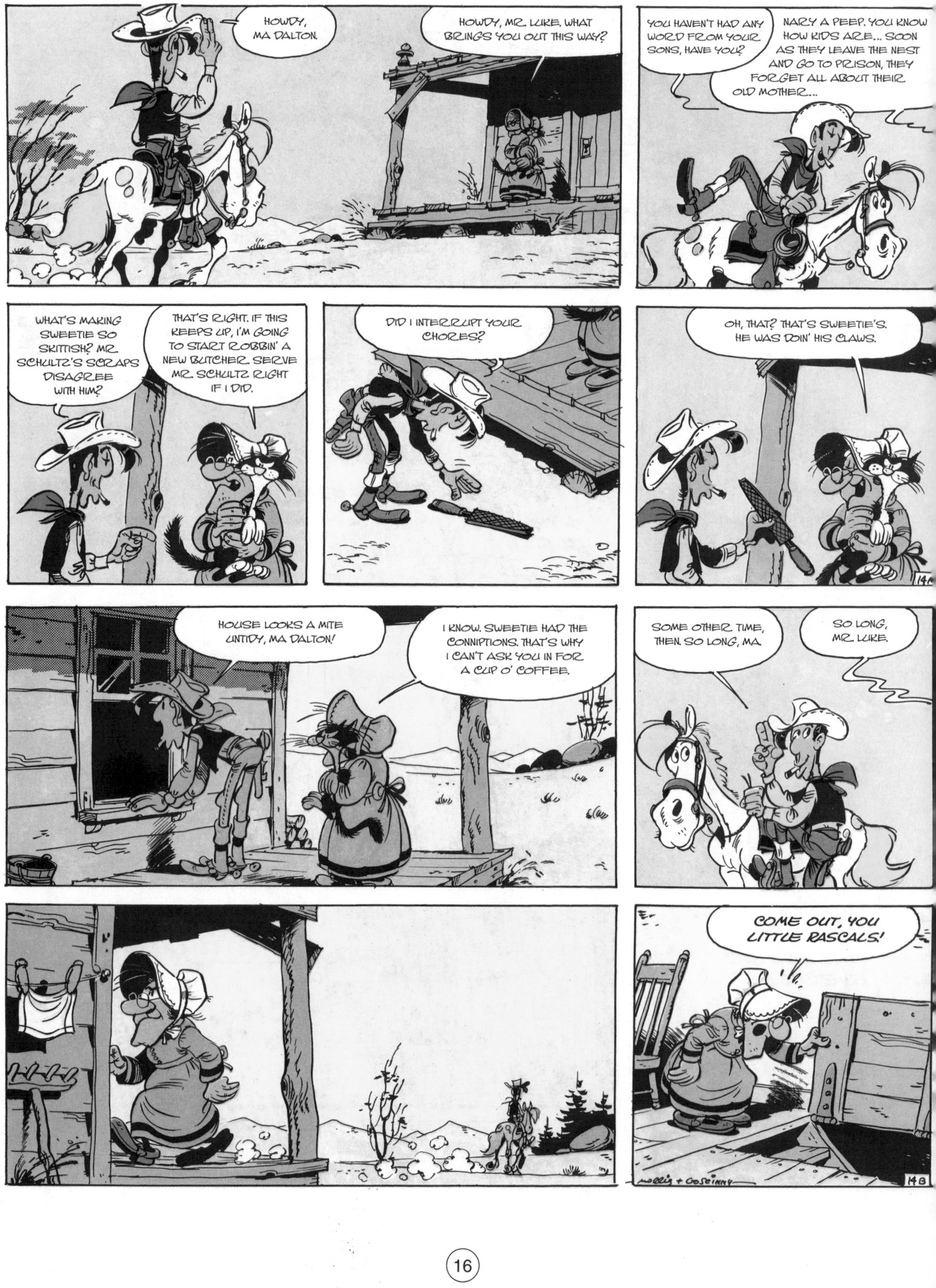
HOWDY, MA DALTON.
HOWDY, MR. LUKE. WHAT BRINGS YOU OUT THIS WAY?
YOU HAVEN'T HAD ANY WORD FROM YOUR SONS, HAVE YOU?
NARY A PEEP. YOU KNOW HOW KIDS ARE... SOON AS THEY LEAVE THE NEST AND GO TO PRISON, THEY FORGET ALL ABOUT THEIR OLD MOTHER...
WHAT'S MAKING SWEETIE SO SKITTISH? MR. SCHULTZ'S SCRAPS DISAGREE WITH HIM?
THAT'S RIGHT. IF THIS KEEPS UP, I'M GOING TO START ROBBIN' A NEW BUTCHER. SERVE MR. SCHULTZ RIGHT IF I DID.
DID I INTERRUPT YOUR CHORES?
OH, THAT? THAT'S SWEETIE'S. HE WAS DOIN' HIS CLAWS.
HOUSE LOOKS A MITE UNTIDY, MA DALTON!
I KNOW. SWEETIE HAD THE CONNIPTIONS. THAT'S WHY I CAN'T ASK YOU IN FOR A CUP O' COFFEE.
SOME OTHER TIME, THEN. SO LONG, MA.
SO LONG, MR. LUKE.
COME OUT, YOU LITTLE RASCALS!
MORRIS + GOSCINNY

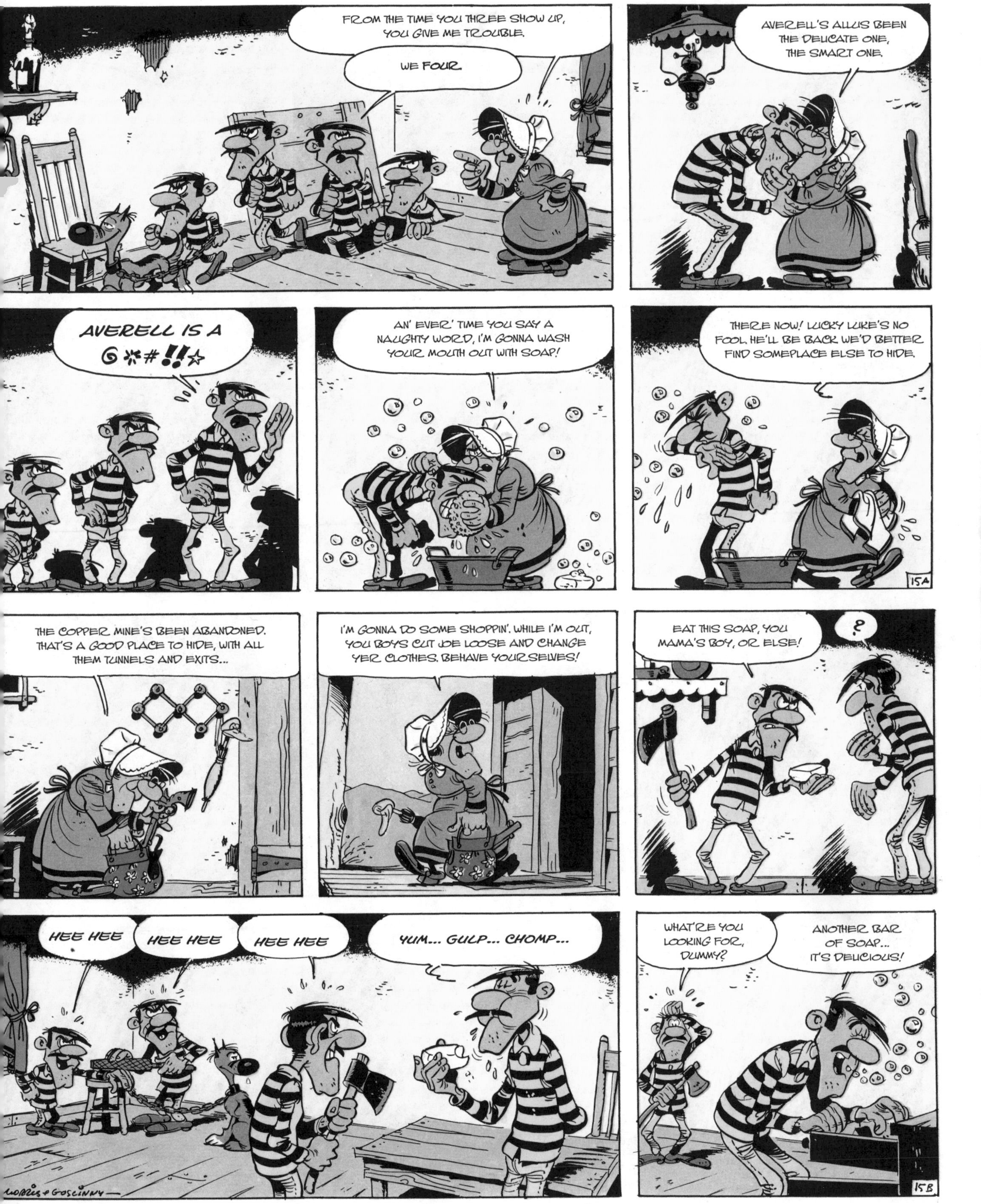
FROM THE TIME YOU THREE SHOW UP, YOU GIVE ME TROUBLE.
WE FOUR
AVERELL'S ALLUS BEEN THE DELICATE ONE, THE SMART ONE.
AVERELL IS A
AN' EVER' TIME YOU SAY A NAUGHTY WORD, I'M GONNA WASH YOUR MOUTH OUT WITH SOAP!
THERE NOW! LUCKY LUKE'S NO FOOL. HE'LL BE BACK WE'D BETTER FIND SOMEPLACE ELSE TO HIDE.
THE COPPER MINE'S BEEN ABANDONED. THAT'S A GOOD PLACE TO HIDE, WITH ALL THEM TUNNELS AND EXITS...
I'M GONNA DO SOME SHOPPIN'. WHILE I'M OUT, YOU BOYS CUT JOE LOOSE AND CHANGE YER CLOTHES. BEHAVE YOURSELVES!
EAT THIS SOAP, YOU MAMA'S BOY, OR ELSE!
?
HEE HEE
HEE HEE
HEE HEE
YUM... GULP... CHOMP...
WHAT'RE YOU LOOKING FOR, DUMMY?
ANOTHER BAR OF SOAP... IT'S DELICIOUS!

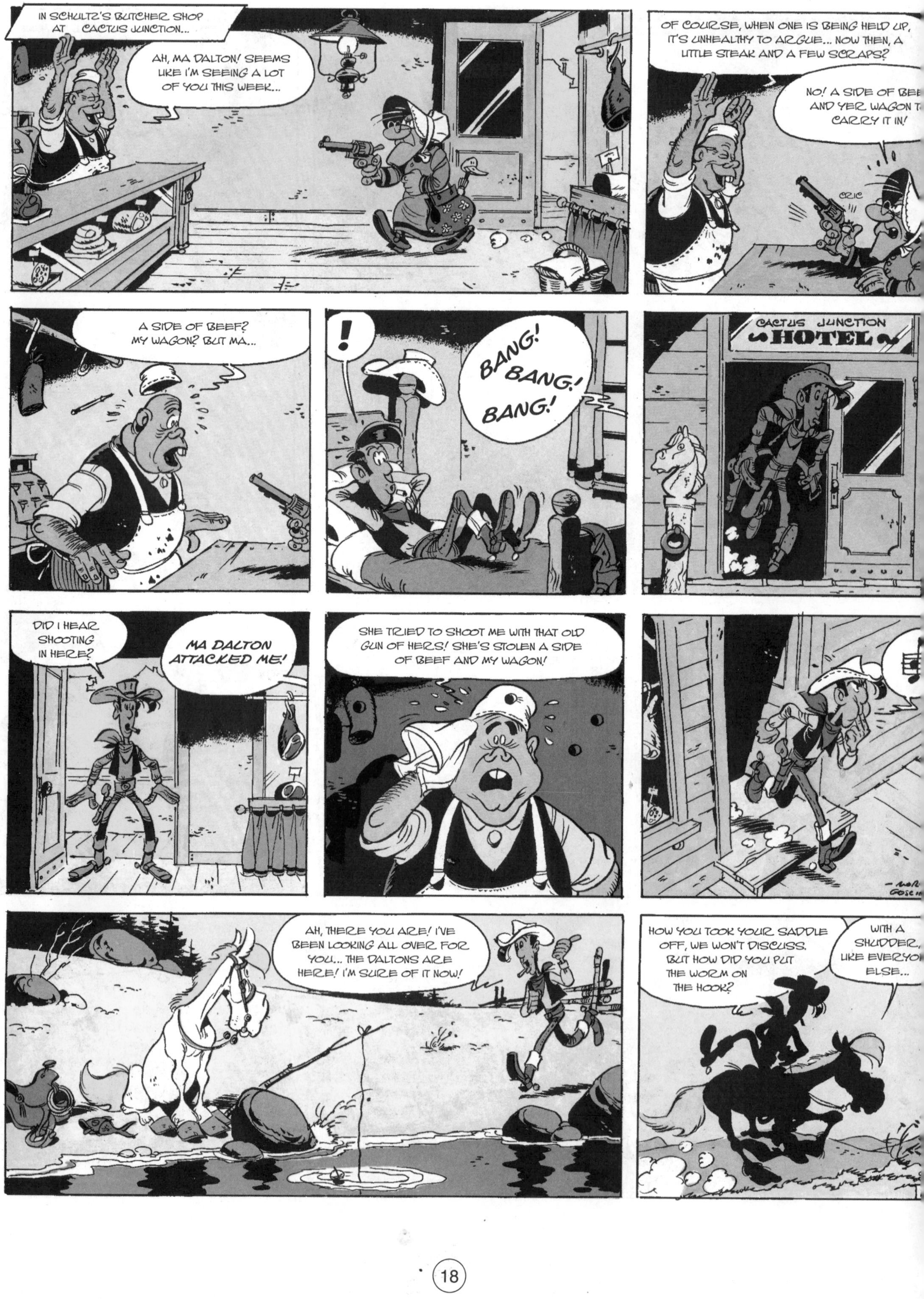

IN SCHULTZ'S BUTCHER SHOP AT CACTUS JUNCTION...
AH, MA DALTON! SEEMS LIKE I'M SEEING A LOT OF YOU THIS WEEK...
OF COURSE, WHEN ONE IS BEING HELD UP, IT'S UNHEALTHY TO ARGUE... NOW THEN, A LITTLE STEAK AND A FEW SCRAPS?
NO! A SIDE OF BEE AND YER WAGON T CARRY IT IN!
CRIC
A SIDE OF BEEF? MY WAGON? BUT MA...
!
BANG! BANG! BANG!
CACTUS JUNCTION HOTEL
DID I HEAR SHOOTING IN HERE?
MA DALTON ATTACKED ME!
SHE TRIED TO SHOOT ME WITH THAT OLD GUN OF HERS! SHE'S STOLEN A SIDE OF BEEF AND MY WAGON!
AH, THERE YOU ARE! I'VE BEEN LOOKING ALL OVER FOR YOU... THE DALTONS ARE HERE! I'M SURE OF IT NOW!
HOW YOU TOOK YOUR SADDLE OFF, WE WON'T DISCUSS. BUT HOW DID YOU PUT THE WORM ON THE HOOK?
WITH A SHUDDER, LIKE EVERYO ELSE...

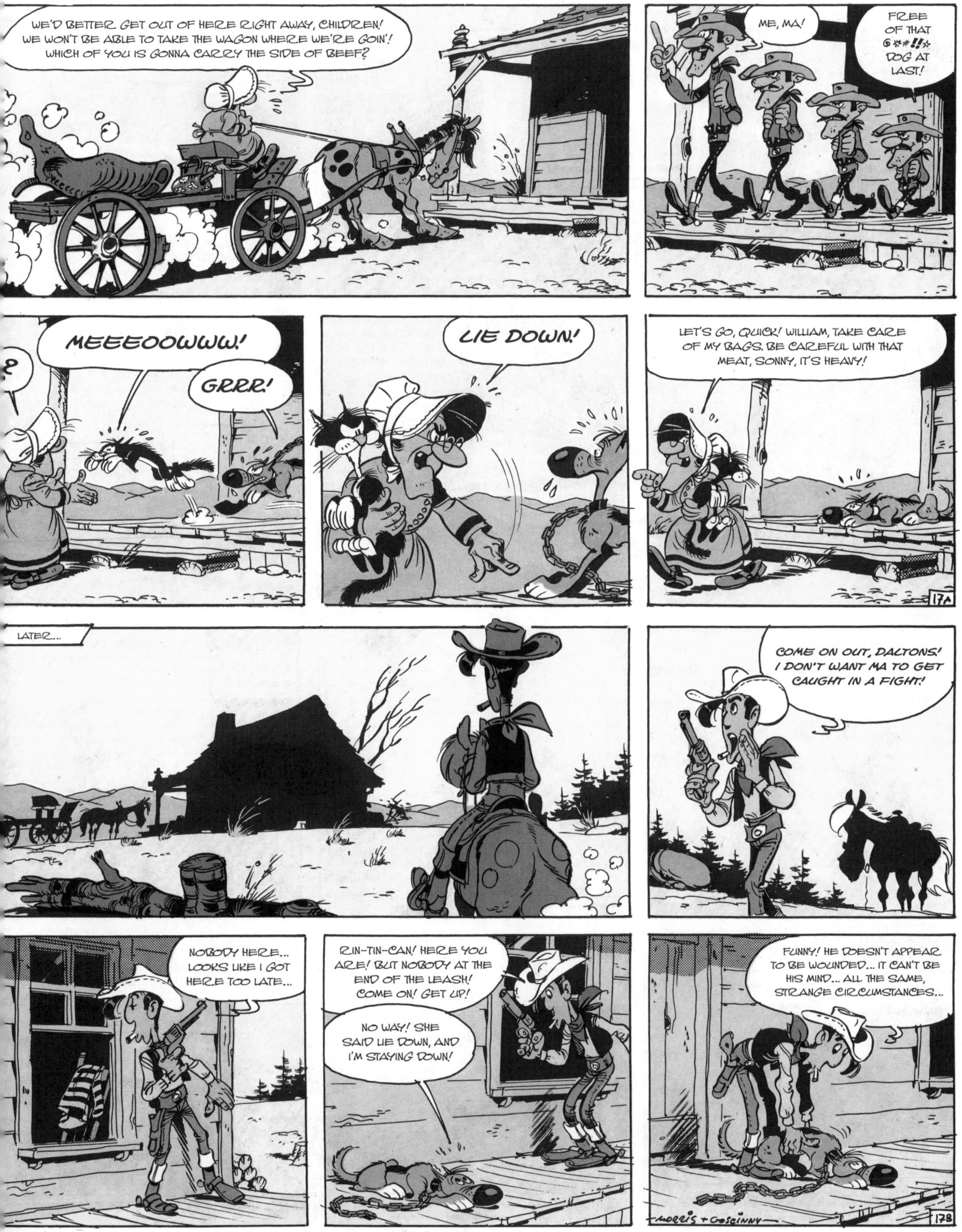
WE'D BETTER GET OUT OF HERE RIGHT AWAY, CHILDREN! WE WON'T BE ABLE TO TAKE THE WAGON WHERE WE'RE GOIN'! WHICH OF YOU IS GONNA CARRY THE SIDE OF BEEF?
ME, MA!
FREE OF THAT @*#!!* DOG AT LAST!
MEEEOOWWW!
GRRR!
LIE DOWN!
LET'S GO, QUICK! WILLIAM, TAKE CARE OF MY BAGS. BE CAREFUL WITH THAT MEAT, SONNY, IT'S HEAVY!
17A
LATER...
COME ON OUT, DALTONS! I DON'T WANT MA TO GET CAUGHT IN A FIGHT!
NOBODY HERE... LOOKS LIKE I GOT HERE TOO LATE...
RIN-TIN-CAN! HERE YOU ARE! BUT NOBODY AT THE END OF THE LEASH! COME ON! GET UP!
NO WAY! SHE SAID LIE DOWN, AND I'M STAYING DOWN!
FUNNY! HE DOESN'T APPEAR TO BE WOUNDED... IT CAN'T BE HIS MIND... ALL THE SAME, STRANGE CIRCUMSTANCES...
MORRIS + GOSCINNY
17B

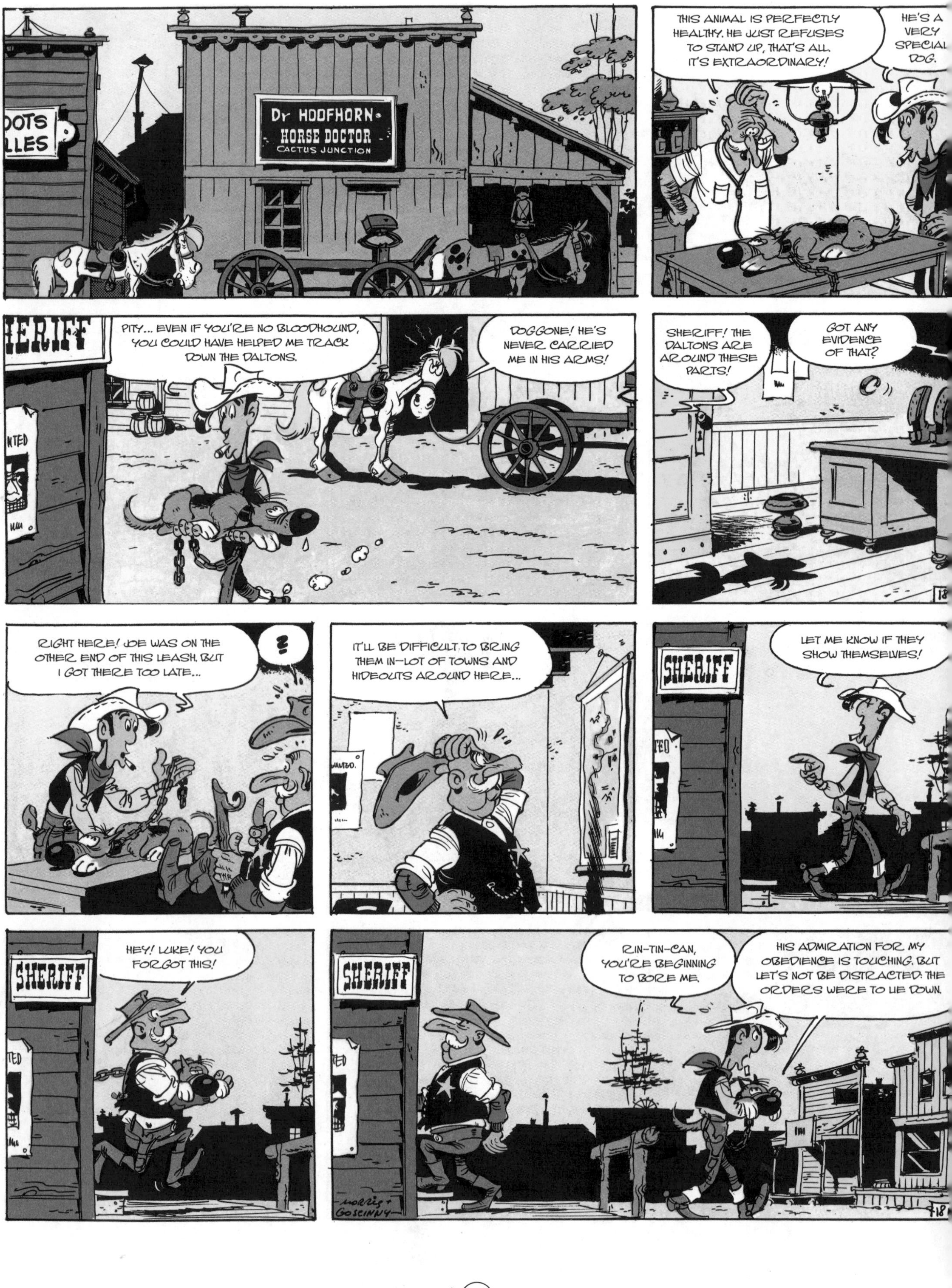
Dr HOOFHORN
HORSE DOCTOR
CACTUS JUNCTION
THIS ANIMAL IS PERFECTLY HEALTHY. HE JUST REFUSES TO STAND UP, THAT'S ALL. IT'S EXTRAORDINARY!
HE'S A VERY SPECIAL DOG.
SHERIFF
PITY... EVEN IF YOU'RE NO BLOODHOUND, YOU COULD HAVE HELPED ME TRACK DOWN THE DALTONS.
DOGGONE! HE'S NEVER CARRIED ME IN HIS ARMS!
SHERIFF! THE DALTONS ARE AROUND THESE PARTS!
GOT ANY EVIDENCE OF THAT?
RIGHT HERE! JOE WAS ON THE OTHER END OF THIS LEASH, BUT I GOT THERE TOO LATE...
IT'LL BE DIFFICULT TO BRING THEM IN-LOT OF TOWNS AND HIDEOUTS AROUND HERE...
SHERIFF
LET ME KNOW IF THEY SHOW THEMSELVES!
SHERIFF
HEY! LUKE! YOU FORGOT THIS!
SHERIFF
RIN-TIN-CAN, YOU'RE BEGINNING TO BORE ME.
HIS ADMIRATION FOR MY OBEDIENCE IS TOUCHING, BUT LET'S NOT BE DISTRACTED: THE ORDERS WERE TO LIE DOWN.
MORRIS + GOSCINNY

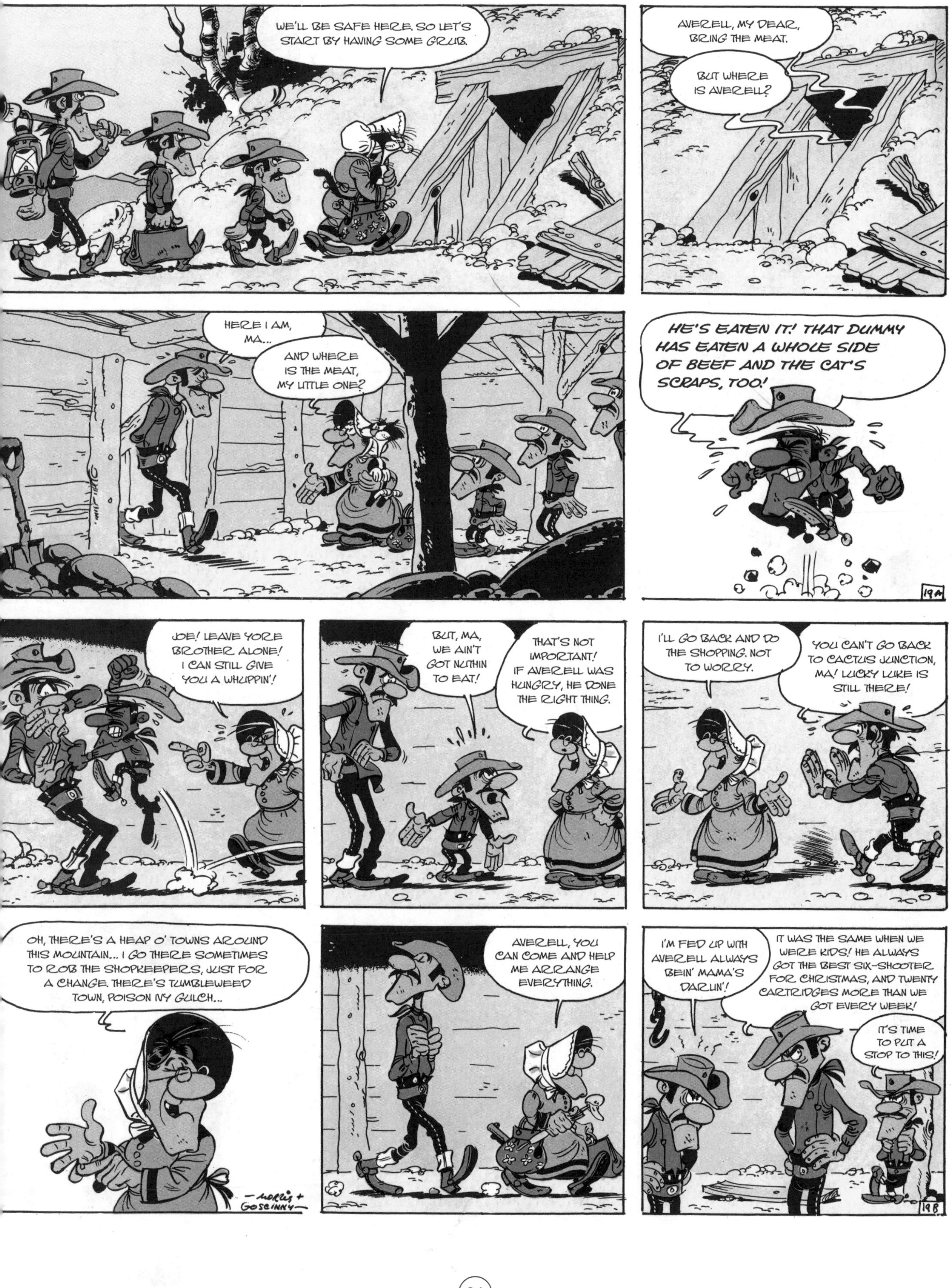
WE'LL BE SAFE HERE. SO LET'S START BY HAVING SOME GRUB.
AVERELL, MY DEAR, BRING THE MEAT.
BUT WHERE IS AVERELL?
HERE I AM, MA...
AND WHERE IS THE MEAT, MY LITTLE ONE?
HE'S EATEN IT! THAT DUMMY HAS EATEN A WHOLE SIDE OF BEEF AND THE CAT'S SCRAPS, TOO!
JOE! LEAVE YORE BROTHER ALONE! I CAN STILL GIVE YOU A WHUPPIN'!
BUT, MA, WE AIN'T GOT NUTHIN TO EAT!
THAT'S NOT IMPORTANT! IF AVERELL WAS HUNGRY, HE DONE THE RIGHT THING.
I'LL GO BACK AND DO THE SHOPPING. NOT TO WORRY.
YOU CAN'T GO BACK TO CACTUS JUNCTION, MA! LUCKY LUKE IS STILL THERE!
OH, THERE'S A HEAP O' TOWNS AROUND THIS MOUNTAIN... I GO THERE SOMETIMES TO ROB THE SHOPKEEPERS, JUST FOR A CHANGE. THERE'S TUMBLEWEED TOWN, POISON IVY GULCH...
AVERELL, YOU CAN COME AND HELP ME ARRANGE EVERYTHING.
I'M FED UP WITH AVERELL ALWAYS BEIN' MAMA'S DARLIN'!
IT WAS THE SAME WHEN WE WERE KIDS! HE ALWAYS GOT THE BEST SIX-SHOOTER FOR CHRISTMAS, AND TWENTY CARTRIDGES MORE THAN WE GOT EVERY WEEK!
IT'S TIME TO PUT A STOP TO THIS!

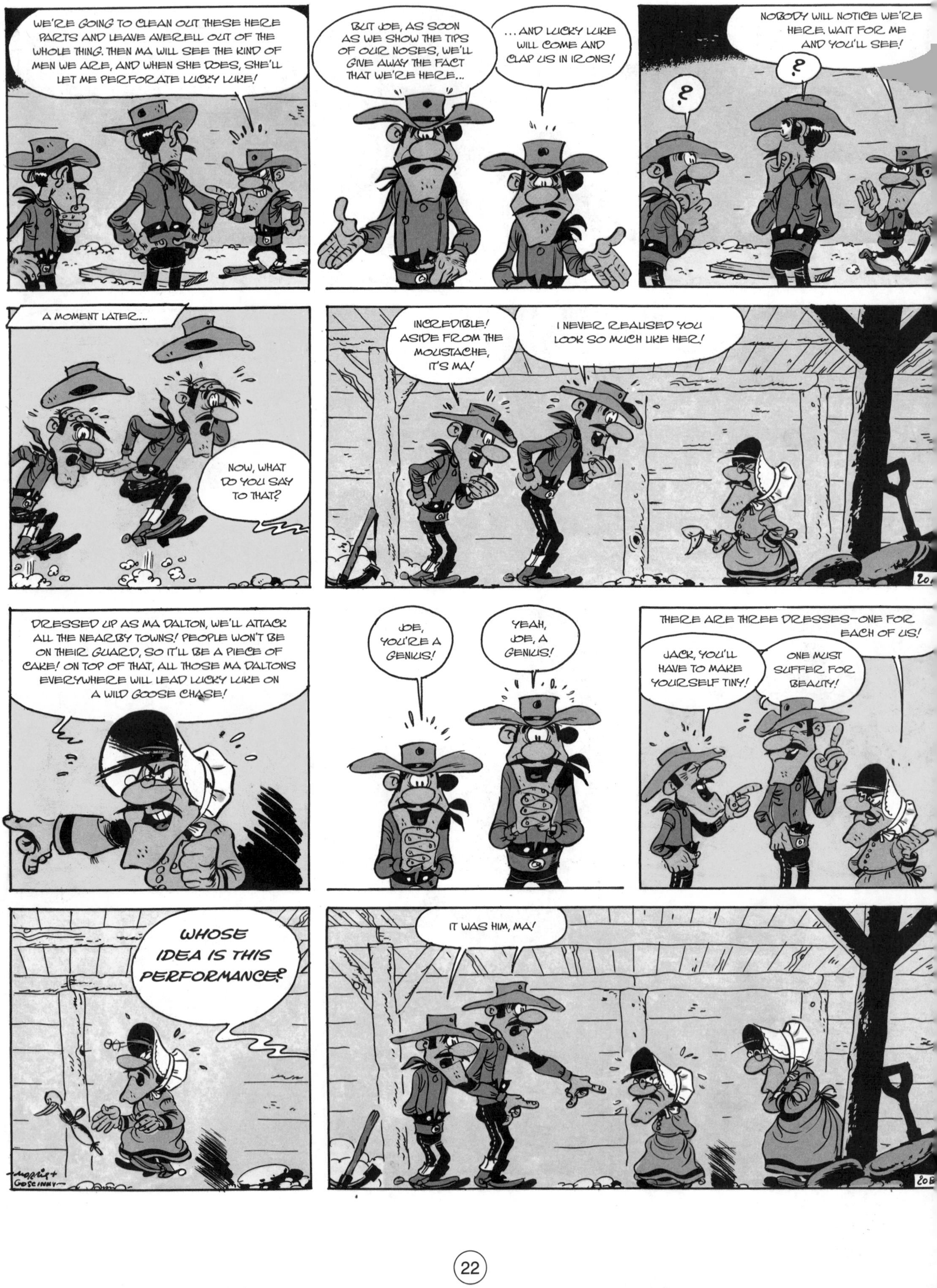

WE'RE GOING TO CLEAN OUT THESE HERE PARTS AND LEAVE AVERELL OUT OF THE WHOLE THING. THEN MA WILL SEE THE KIND OF MEN WE ARE, AND WHEN SHE DOES, SHE'LL LET ME PERFORATE LUCKY LUKE!
BUT JOE, AS SOON AS WE SHOW THE TIPS OF OUR NOSES, WE'LL GIVE AWAY THE FACT THAT WE'RE HERE...
...AND LUCKY LUKE WILL COME AND CLAP US IN IRONS!
NOBODY WILL NOTICE WE'RE HERE. WAIT FOR ME AND YOU'LL SEE!
?
?
A MOMENT LATER...
NOW, WHAT DO YOU SAY TO THAT?
INCREDIBLE! ASIDE FROM THE MOUSTACHE, IT'S MA!
I NEVER REALISED YOU LOOK SO MUCH LIKE HER!
DRESSED UP AS MA DALTON, WE'LL ATTACK ALL THE NEARBY TOWNS! PEOPLE WON'T BE ON THEIR GUARD, SO IT'LL BE A PIECE OF CAKE! ON TOP OF THAT, ALL THOSE MA DALTONS EVERYWHERE WILL LEAD LUCKY LUKE ON A WILD GOOSE CHASE!
JOE, YOU'RE A GENIUS!
YEAH, JOE, A GENIUS!
THERE ARE THREE DRESSES—ONE FOR EACH OF US!
JACK, YOU'LL HAVE TO MAKE YOURSELF TINY!
ONE MUST SUFFER FOR BEAUTY!
WHOSE IDEA IS THIS PERFORMANCE?
MORRIS + GOSCINNY
IT WAS HIM, MA!

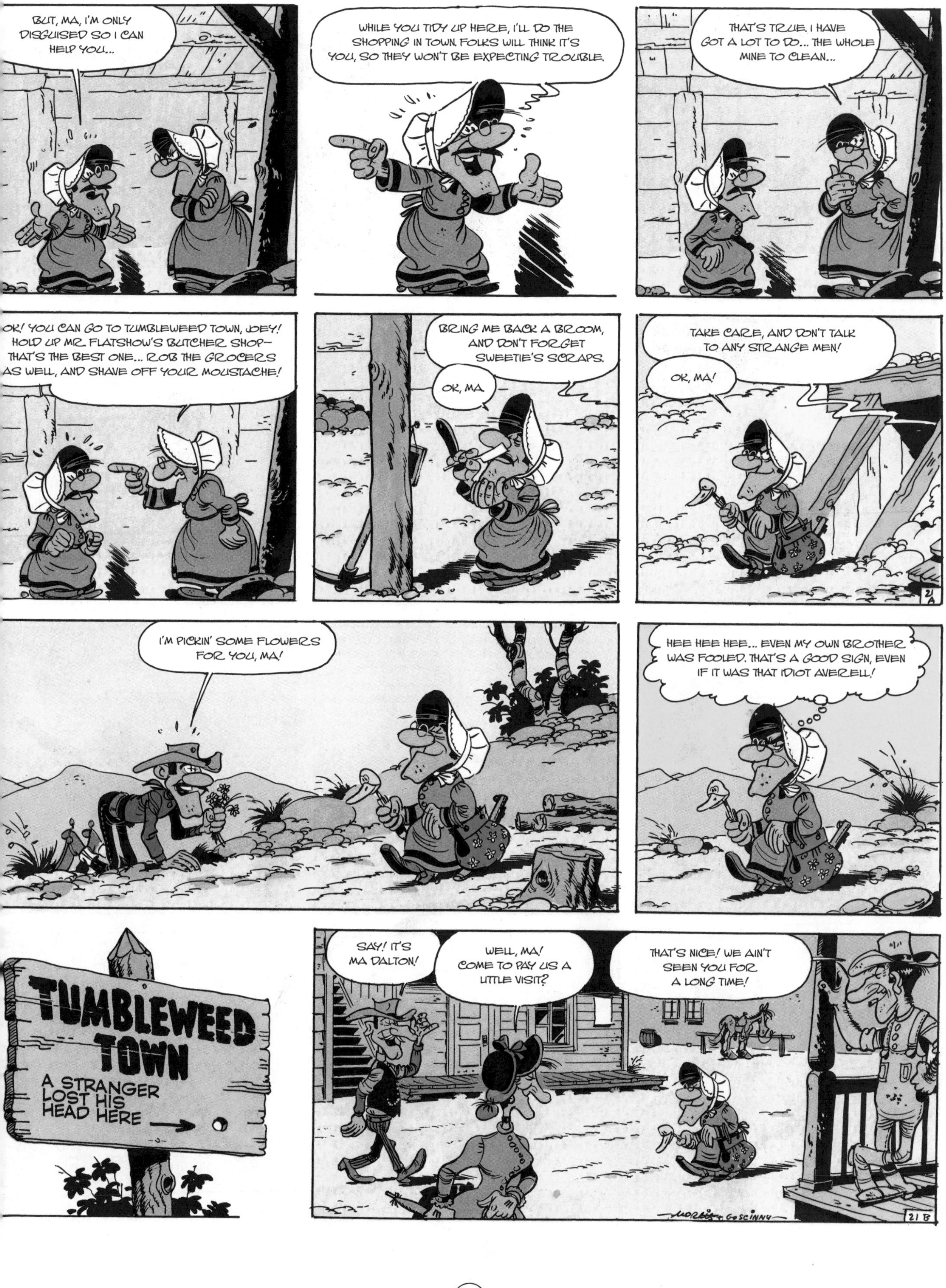
BUT, MA, I'M ONLY DISGUISED SO I CAN HELP YOU...
WHILE YOU TIDY UP HERE, I'LL DO THE SHOPPING IN TOWN. FOLKS WILL THINK IT'S YOU, SO THEY WON'T BE EXPECTING TROUBLE.
THAT'S TRUE. I HAVE GOT A LOT TO DO... THE WHOLE MINE TO CLEAN...
OK! YOU CAN GO TO TUMBLEWEED TOWN, JOEY! HOLD UP MR. FLATSHOW'S BUTCHER SHOP– THAT'S THE BEST ONE... ROB THE GROCERS AS WELL, AND SHAVE OFF YOUR MOUSTACHE!
BRING ME BACK A BROOM, AND DON'T FORGET SWEETIE'S SCRAPS.
OK, MA
TAKE CARE, AND DON'T TALK TO ANY STRANGE MEN!
OK, MA!
21 A
I'M PICKIN' SOME FLOWERS FOR YOU, MA!
HEE HEE HEE... EVEN MY OWN BROTHER WAS FOOLED. THAT'S A GOOD SIGN, EVEN IF IT WAS THAT IDIOT AVERELL!
TUMBLEWEED TOWN
A STRANGER LOST HIS HEAD HERE
SAY! IT'S MA DALTON!
WELL, MA! COME TO PAY US A LITTLE VISIT?
THAT'S NICE! WE AIN'T SEEN YOU FOR A LONG TIME!
MORRIS + GOSCINNY
21 B

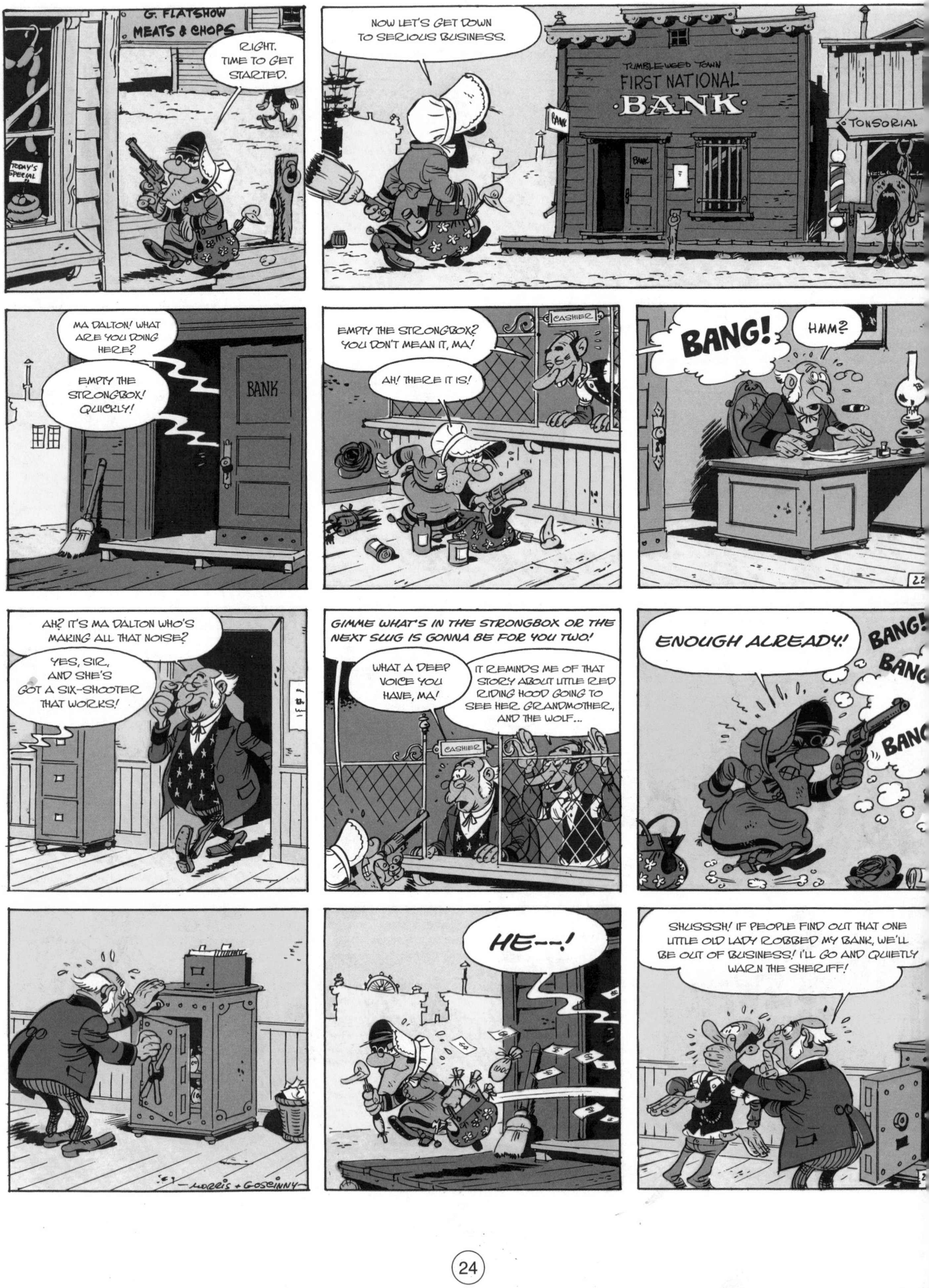
G. FLATSHOW MEATS & CHOPS
TODAY'S SPECIAL
RIGHT. TIME TO GET STARTED.
NOW LET'S GET DOWN TO SERIOUS BUSINESS.
TUMBLEWEED TOWN FIRST NATIONAL ·BANK·
BANK
TONSORIAL
MA DALTON! WHAT ARE YOU DOING HERE?
EMPTY THE STRONGBOX! QUICKLY!
BANK
EMPTY THE STRONGBOX? YOU DON'T MEAN IT, MA!
CASHIER
AH! THERE IT IS!
BANG!
HMM?
AH? IT'S MA DALTON WHO'S MAKING ALL THAT NOISE?
YES, SIR, AND SHE'S GOT A SIX-SHOOTER THAT WORKS!
GIMME WHAT'S IN THE STRONGBOX OR THE NEXT SLUG IS GONNA BE FOR YOU TWO!
WHAT A DEEP VOICE YOU HAVE, MA!
IT REMINDS ME OF THAT STORY ABOUT LITTLE RED RIDING HOOD GOING TO SEE HER GRANDMOTHER, AND THE WOLF...
CASHIER
ENOUGH ALREADY!
BANG!
BANG
BANG
MORRIS + GOSCINNY
HE--!
SHUSSSH! IF PEOPLE FIND OUT THAT ONE LITTLE OLD LADY ROBBED MY BANK, WE'LL BE OUT OF BUSINESS! I'LL GO AND QUIETLY WARN THE SHERIFF!

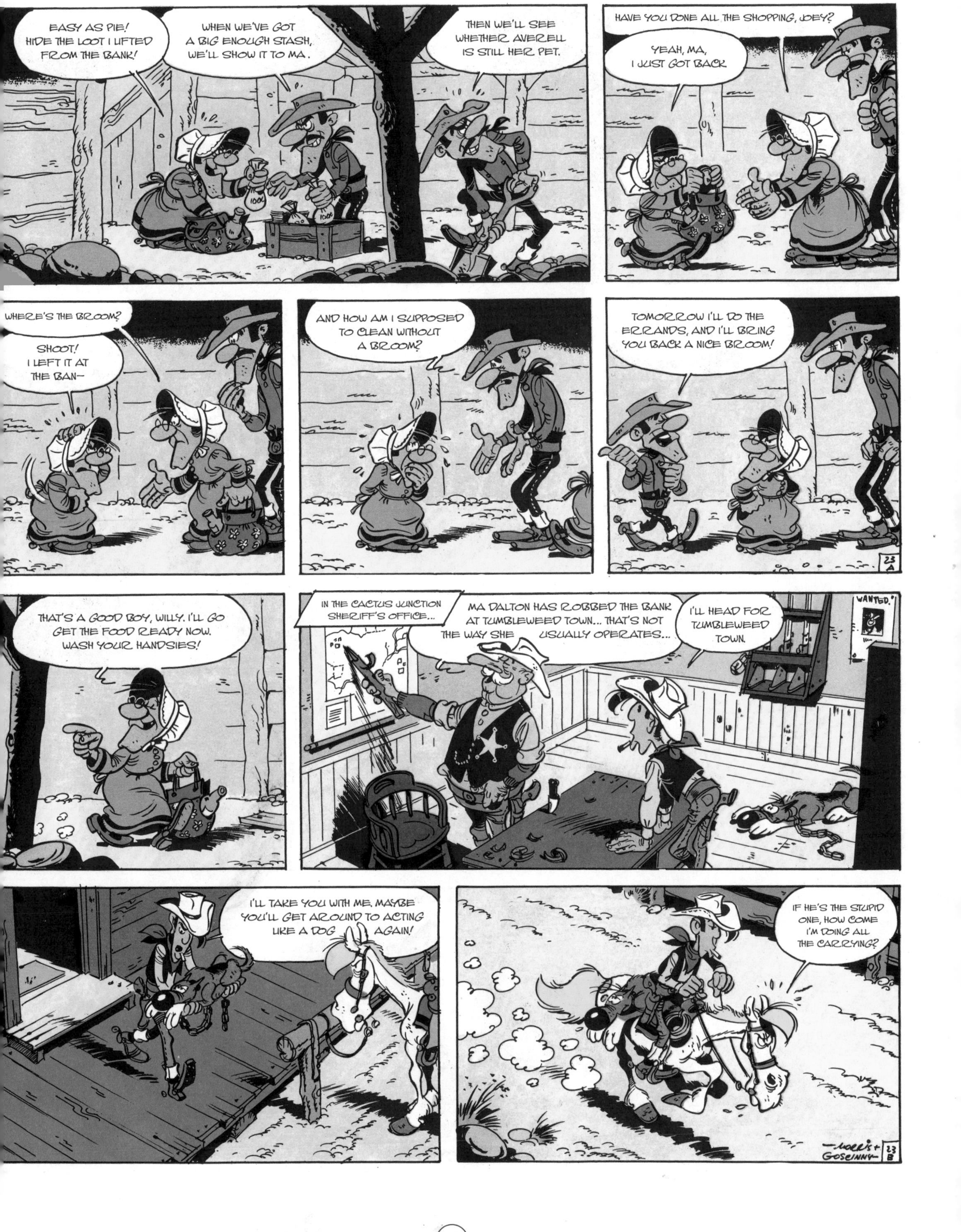
EASY AS PIE! HIDE THE LOOT I LIFTED FROM THE BANK!
WHEN WE'VE GOT A BIG ENOUGH STASH, WE'LL SHOW IT TO MA.
THEN WE'LL SEE WHETHER AVERELL IS STILL HER PET.
HAVE YOU DONE ALL THE SHOPPING, JOEY?
YEAH, MA, I JUST GOT BACK
WHERE'S THE BROOM?
SHOOT! I LEFT IT AT THE BAN–
AND HOW AM I SUPPOSED TO CLEAN WITHOUT A BROOM?
TOMORROW I'LL DO THE ERRANDS, AND I'LL BRING YOU BACK A NICE BROOM!
23 A
THAT'S A GOOD BOY, WILLY. I'LL GO GET THE FOOD READY NOW. WASH YOUR HANDSIES!
IN THE CACTUS JUNCTION SHERIFF'S OFFICE...
MA DALTON HAS ROBBED THE BANK AT TUMBLEWEED TOWN... THAT'S NOT THE WAY SHE USUALLY OPERATES...
I'LL HEAD FOR TUMBLEWEED TOWN.
WANTED
I'LL TAKE YOU WITH ME. MAYBE YOU'LL GET AROUND TO ACTING LIKE A DOG AGAIN!
IF HE'S THE STUPID ONE, HOW COME I'M DOING ALL THE CARRYING?
MORRIS + GOSCINNY
23 B

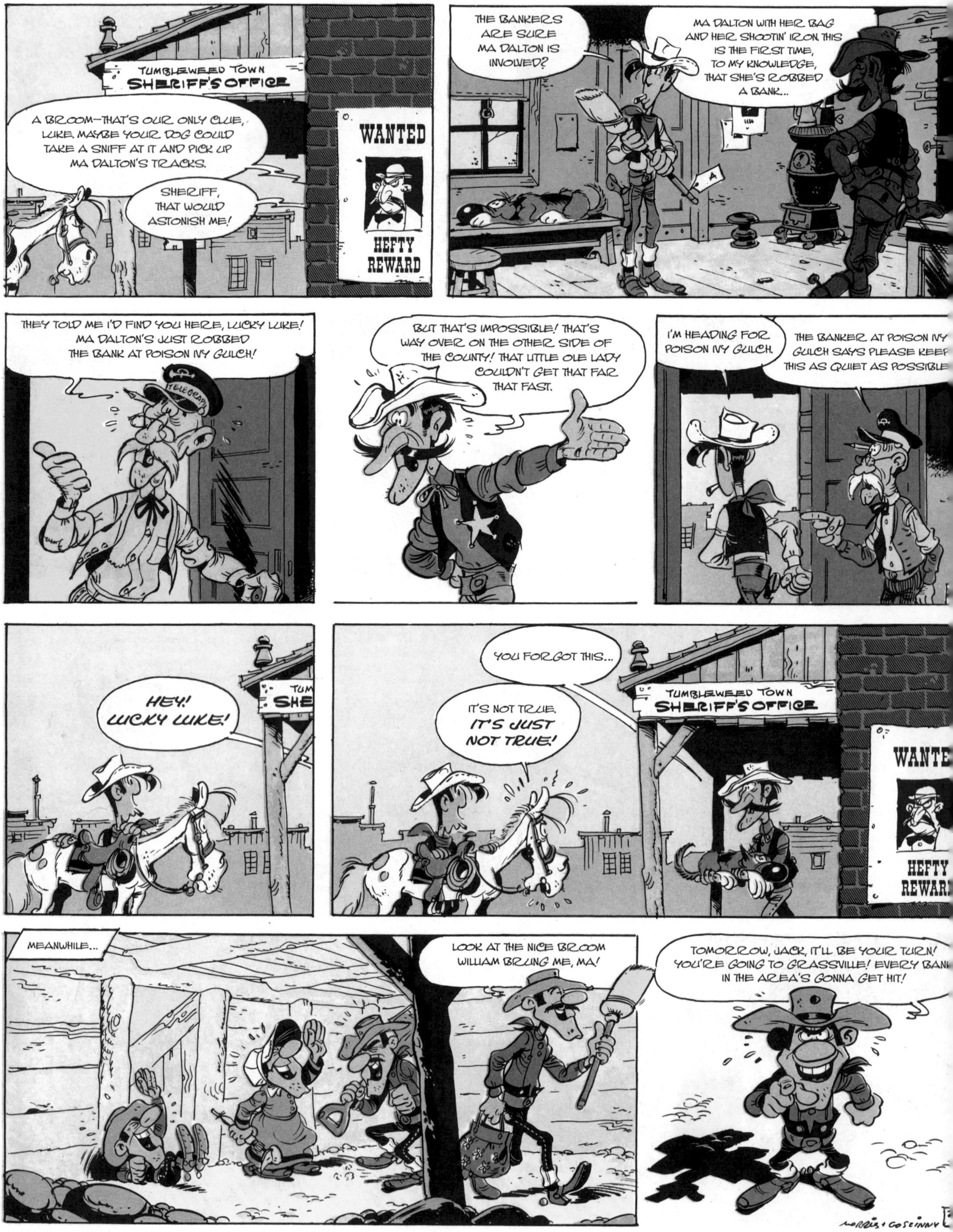

TUMBLEWEED TOWN
SHERIFF'S OFFICE
A BROOM—THAT'S OUR ONLY CLUE, LUKE. MAYBE YOUR DOG COULD TAKE A SNIFF AT IT AND PICK UP MA DALTON'S TRACKS.
SHERIFF, THAT WOULD ASTONISH ME!
WANTED
HEFTY REWARD
THE BANKERS ARE SURE MA DALTON IS INVOLVED?
MA DALTON WITH HER BAG AND HER SHOOTIN' IRON. THIS IS THE FIRST TIME, TO MY KNOWLEDGE, THAT SHE'S ROBBED A BANK...
A
THEY TOLD ME I'D FIND YOU HERE, LUCKY LUKE! MA DALTON'S JUST ROBBED THE BANK AT POISON IVY GULCH!
TELEGRAPH
BUT THAT'S IMPOSSIBLE! THAT'S WAY OVER ON THE OTHER SIDE OF THE COUNTY! THAT LITTLE OLE LADY COULDN'T GET THAT FAR THAT FAST.
I'M HEADING FOR POISON IVY GULCH.
THE BANKER AT POISON IVY GULCH SAYS PLEASE KEEP THIS AS QUIET AS POSSIBLE
HEY! LUCKY LUKE!
YOU FORGOT THIS...
IT'S NOT TRUE. IT'S JUST NOT TRUE!
TUMBLEWEED TOWN
SHERIFF'S OFFICE
HEFTY
MEANWHILE...
LOOK AT THE NICE BROOM WILLIAM BRUNG ME, MA!
TOMORROW, JACK, IT'LL BE YOUR TURN! YOU'RE GOING TO GRASSVILLE! EVERY BANK IN THE AREA'S GONNA GET HIT!
MORRIS + GOSCINNY

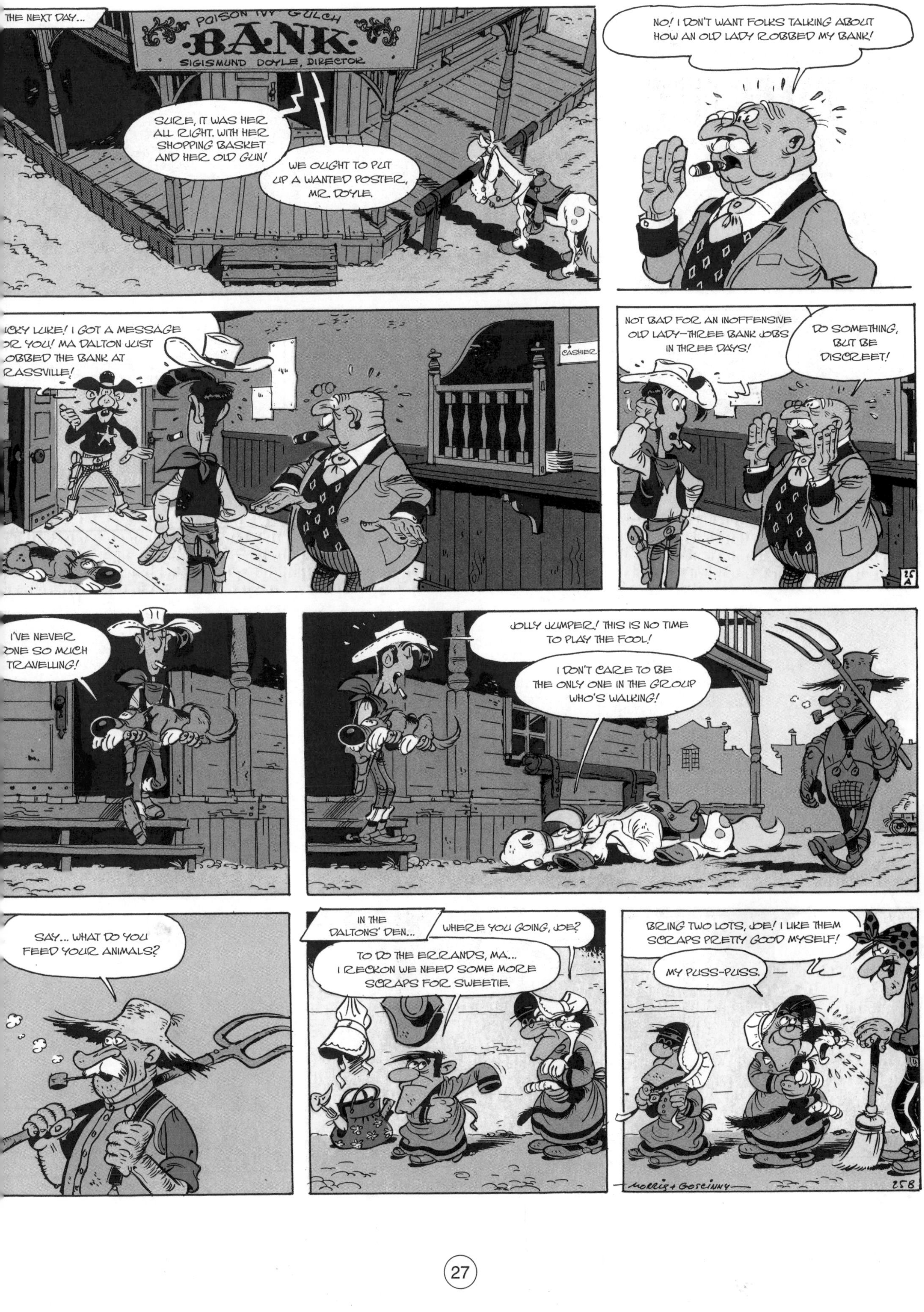
THE NEXT DAY...
POISON IVY GULCH BANK SIGISMUND DOYLE, DIRECTOR
SURE, IT WAS HER ALL RIGHT, WITH HER SHOPPING BASKET AND HER OLD GUN!
WE OUGHT TO PUT UP A WANTED POSTER, MR DOYLE.
NO! I DON'T WANT FOLKS TALKING ABOUT HOW AN OLD LADY ROBBED MY BANK!
ICKY LUKE! I GOT A MESSAGE OR YOU! MA DALTON JUST OBBED THE BANK AT RASSVILLE!
CASHIER
NOT BAD FOR AN INOFFENSIVE OLD LADY—THREE BANK JOBS IN THREE DAYS!
DO SOMETHING, BUT BE DISCREET!
25A
I'VE NEVER ONE SO MUCH TRAVELLING!
JOLLY JUMPER! THIS IS NO TIME TO PLAY THE FOOL!
I DON'T CARE TO BE THE ONLY ONE IN THE GROUP WHO'S WALKING!
SAY... WHAT DO YOU FEED YOUR ANIMALS?
IN THE DALTONS' DEN...
WHERE YOU GOING, JOE?
TO DO THE ERRANDS, MA... I RECKON WE NEED SOME MORE SCRAPS FOR SWEETIE.
BRING TWO LOTS, JOE! I LIKE THEM SCRAPS PRETTY GOOD MYSELF!
MY PUSS-PUSS.
MORRIS + GOSCINNY
25B

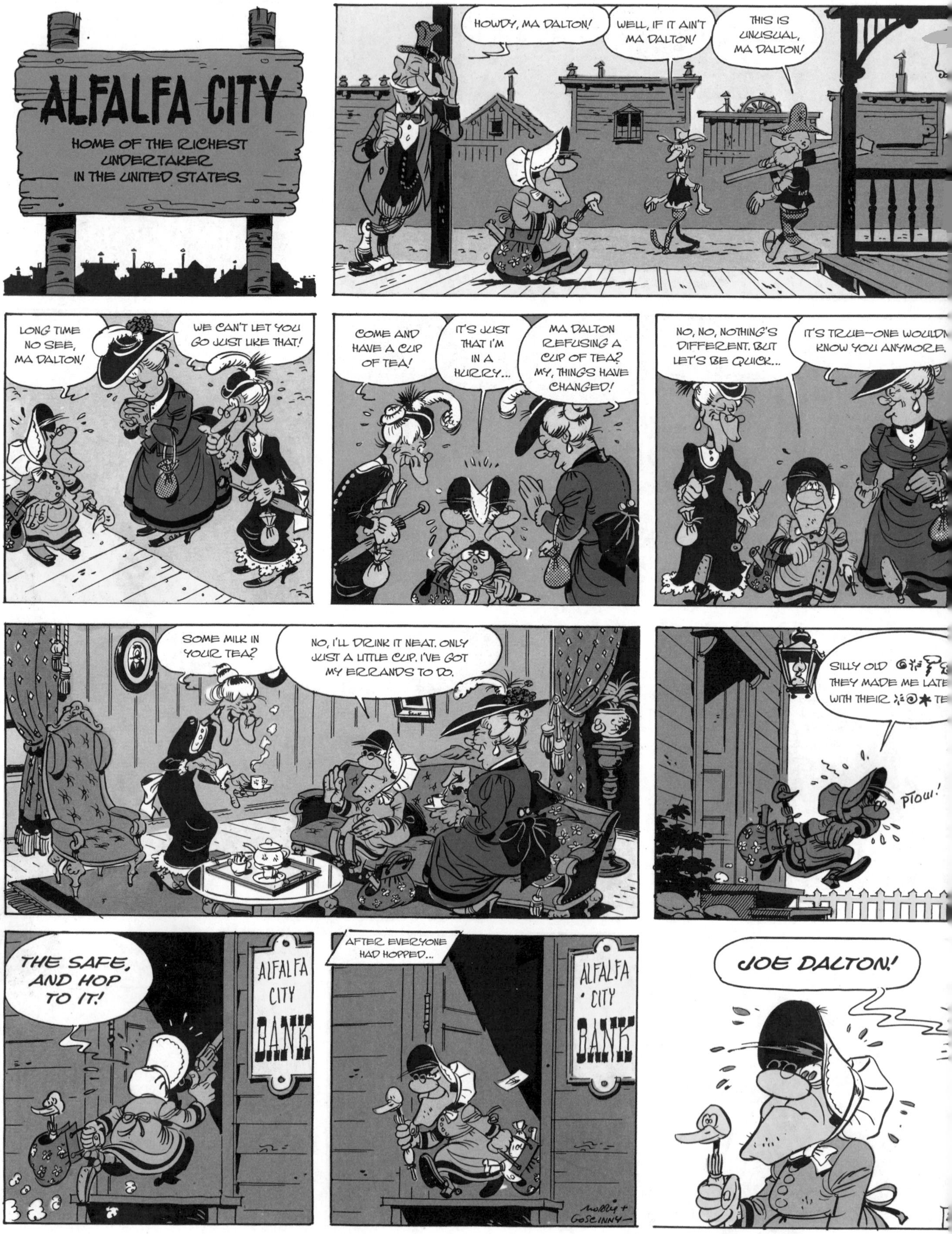
ALFALFA CITY
HOME OF THE RICHEST UNDERTAKER IN THE UNITED STATES.
HOWDY, MA DALTON!
WELL, IF IT AIN'T MA DALTON!
THIS IS UNUSUAL, MA DALTON!
LONG TIME NO SEE, MA DALTON!
WE CAN'T LET YOU GO JUST LIKE THAT!
COME AND HAVE A CUP OF TEA!
IT'S JUST THAT I'M IN A HURRY...
MA DALTON REFUSING A CUP OF TEA? MY, THINGS HAVE CHANGED!
NO, NO, NOTHING'S DIFFERENT. BUT LET'S BE QUICK...
IT'S TRUE—ONE WOULDN' KNOW YOU ANYMORE.
SOME MILK IN YOUR TEA?
NO, I'LL DRINK IT NEAT. ONLY JUST A LITTLE CUP. I'VE GOT MY ERRANDS TO DO.
SILLY OLD
THEY MADE ME LATE
WITH THEIR
PTOUI!
THE SAFE, AND HOP TO IT!
ALFALFA CITY BANK
AFTER EVERYONE HAD HOPPED...
ALFALFA CITY BANK
MORRIS + GOSCINNY
JOE DALTON!

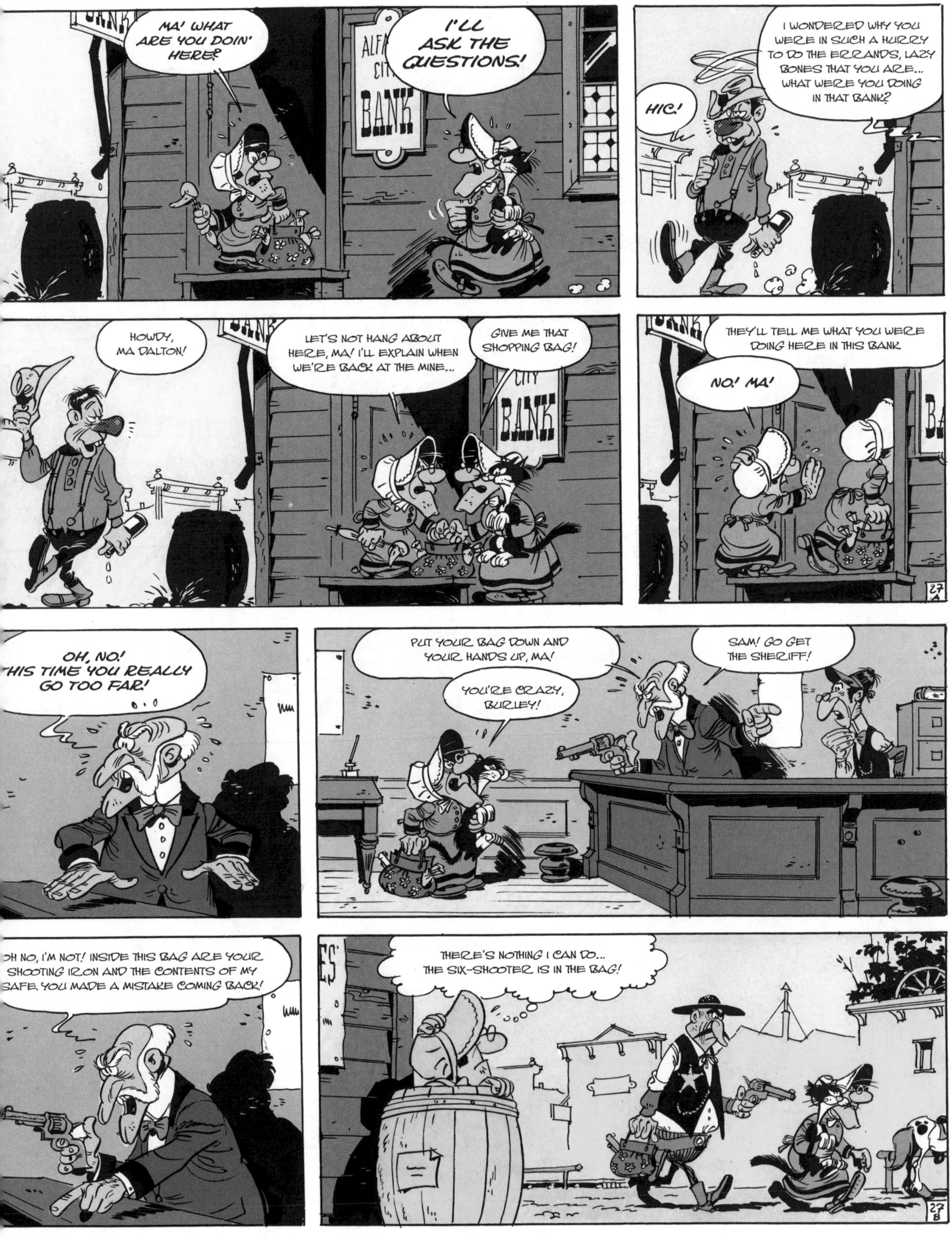

MA! WHAT ARE YOU DOIN' HERE?
I'LL ASK THE QUESTIONS!
ALFA CITY BANK
HIC!
I WONDERED WHY YOU WERE IN SUCH A HURRY TO DO THE ERRANDS, LAZY BONES THAT YOU ARE... WHAT WERE YOU DOING IN THAT BANK?
HOWDY, MA DALTON!
LET'S NOT HANG ABOUT HERE, MA! I'LL EXPLAIN WHEN WE'RE BACK AT THE MINE...
GIVE ME THAT SHOPPING BAG!
BANK
THEY'LL TELL ME WHAT YOU WERE DOING HERE IN THIS BANK
NO! MA!
27 A
OH, NO! THIS TIME YOU REALLY GO TOO FAR!
PUT YOUR BAG DOWN AND YOUR HANDS UP, MA!
YOU'RE CRAZY, BURLEY!
SAM! GO GET THE SHERIFF!
OH NO, I'M NOT! INSIDE THIS BAG ARE YOUR SHOOTING IRON AND THE CONTENTS OF MY SAFE. YOU MADE A MISTAKE COMING BACK!
THERE'S NOTHING I CAN DO... THE SIX-SHOOTER IS IN THE BAG!
27 B

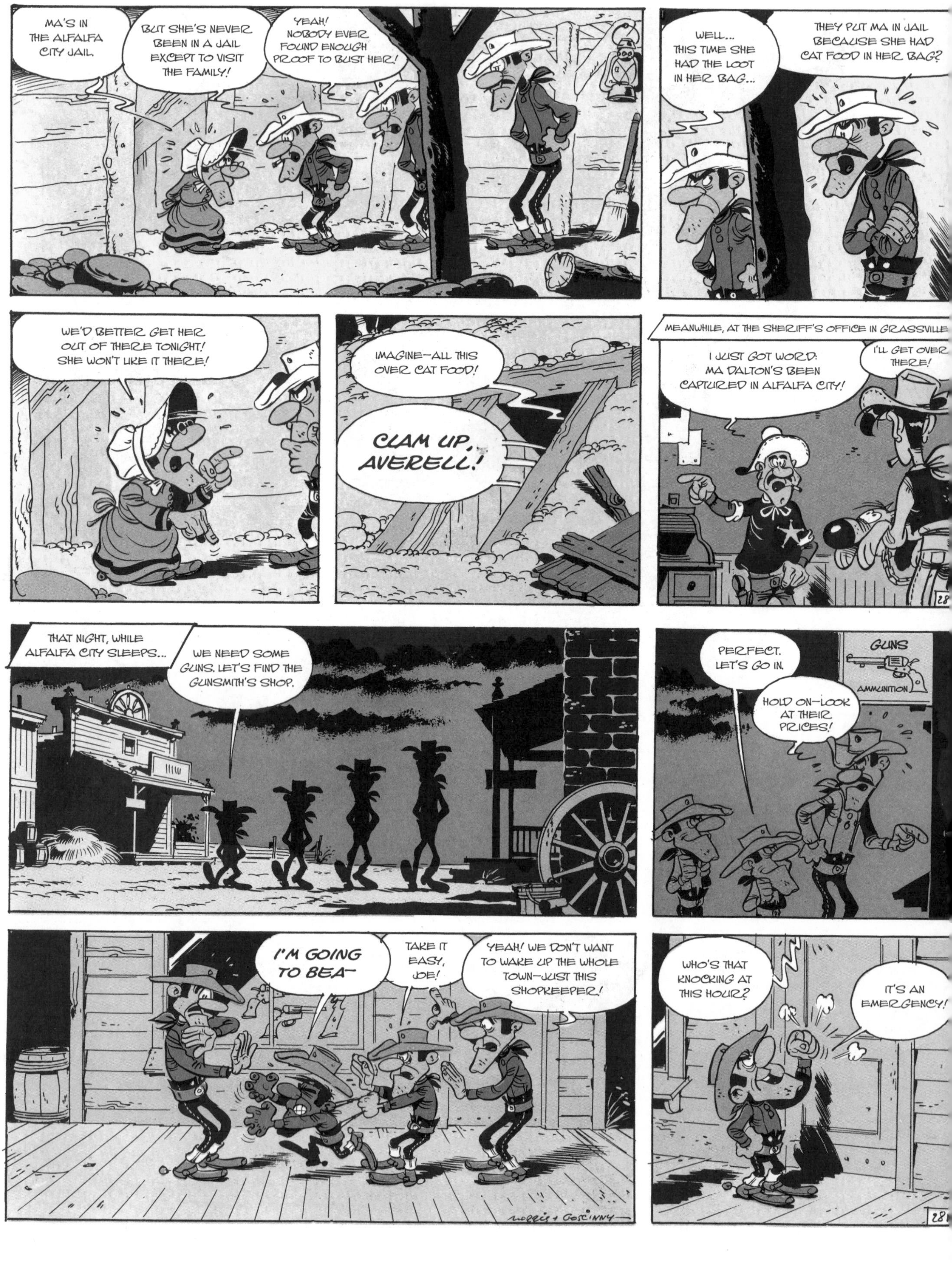
MA'S IN THE ALFALFA CITY JAIL.
BUT SHE'S NEVER BEEN IN A JAIL EXCEPT TO VISIT THE FAMILY!
YEAH! NOBODY EVER FOUND ENOUGH PROOF TO BUST HER!
WELL... THIS TIME SHE HAD THE LOOT IN HER BAG...
THEY PUT MA IN JAIL BECAUSE SHE HAD CAT FOOD IN HER BAG?
WE'D BETTER GET HER OUT OF THERE TONIGHT! SHE WON'T LIKE IT THERE!
IMAGINE—ALL THIS OVER CAT FOOD!
CLAM UP, AVERELL!
MEANWHILE, AT THE SHERIFF'S OFFICE IN GRASSVILLE
I JUST GOT WORD: MA DALTON'S BEEN CAPTURED IN ALFALFA CITY!
I'LL GET OVER THERE!
THAT NIGHT, WHILE ALFALFA CITY SLEEPS...
WE NEED SOME GUNS. LET'S FIND THE GUNSMITH'S SHOP.
GUNS
AMMUNITION
PERFECT. LET'S GO IN.
HOLD ON—LOOK AT THEIR PRICES!
I'M GOING TO BEA—
TAKE IT EASY, JOE!
YEAH! WE DON'T WANT TO WAKE UP THE WHOLE TOWN—JUST THIS SHOPKEEPER!
WHO'S THAT KNOCKING AT THIS HOUR?
IT'S AN EMERGENCY!

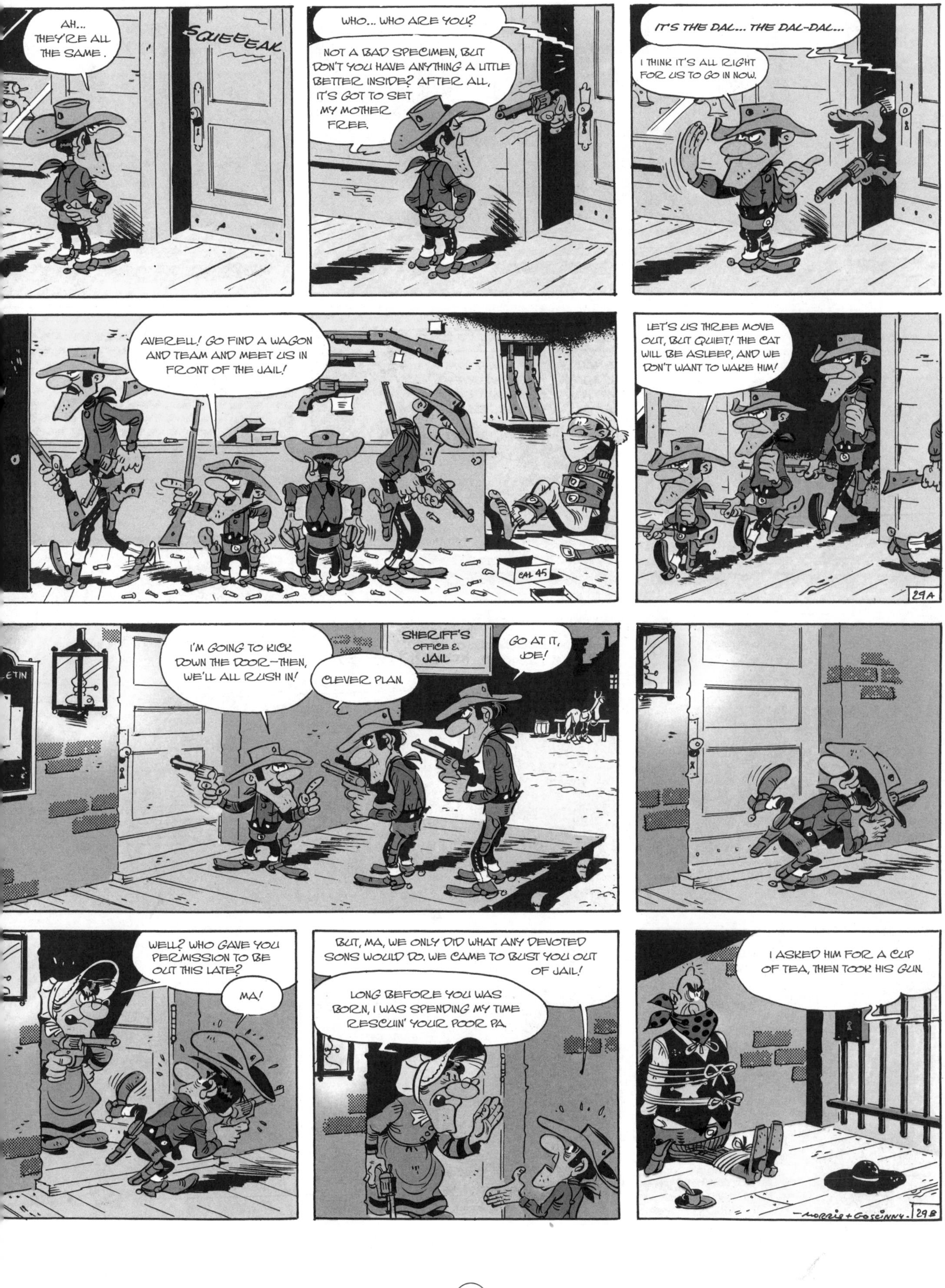
AH... THEY'RE ALL THE SAME.
SQUEEEAK
WHO... WHO ARE YOU?
NOT A BAD SPECIMEN, BUT DON'T YOU HAVE ANYTHING A LITTLE BETTER INSIDE? AFTER ALL, IT'S GOT TO SET MY MOTHER FREE.
IT'S THE DAL... THE DAL-DAL...
I THINK IT'S ALL RIGHT FOR US TO GO IN NOW.
AVERELL! GO FIND A WAGON AND TEAM AND MEET US IN FRONT OF THE JAIL!
CAL 45
LET'S US THREE MOVE OUT, BUT QUIET! THE CAT WILL BE ASLEEP, AND WE DON'T WANT TO WAKE HIM!
29A
SHERIFF'S OFFICE & JAIL
I'M GOING TO KICK DOWN THE DOOR—THEN, WE'LL ALL RUSH IN!
CLEVER PLAN.
GO AT IT, JOE!
WELL? WHO GAVE YOU PERMISSION TO BE OUT THIS LATE?
MA!
BUT, MA, WE ONLY DID WHAT ANY DEVOTED SONS WOULD DO. WE CAME TO BUST YOU OUT OF JAIL!
LONG BEFORE YOU WAS BORN, I WAS SPENDING MY TIME RESCUIN' YOUR POOR PA.
I ASKED HIM FOR A CUP OF TEA, THEN TOOK HIS GUN.
MORRIS + GOSCINNY
29B

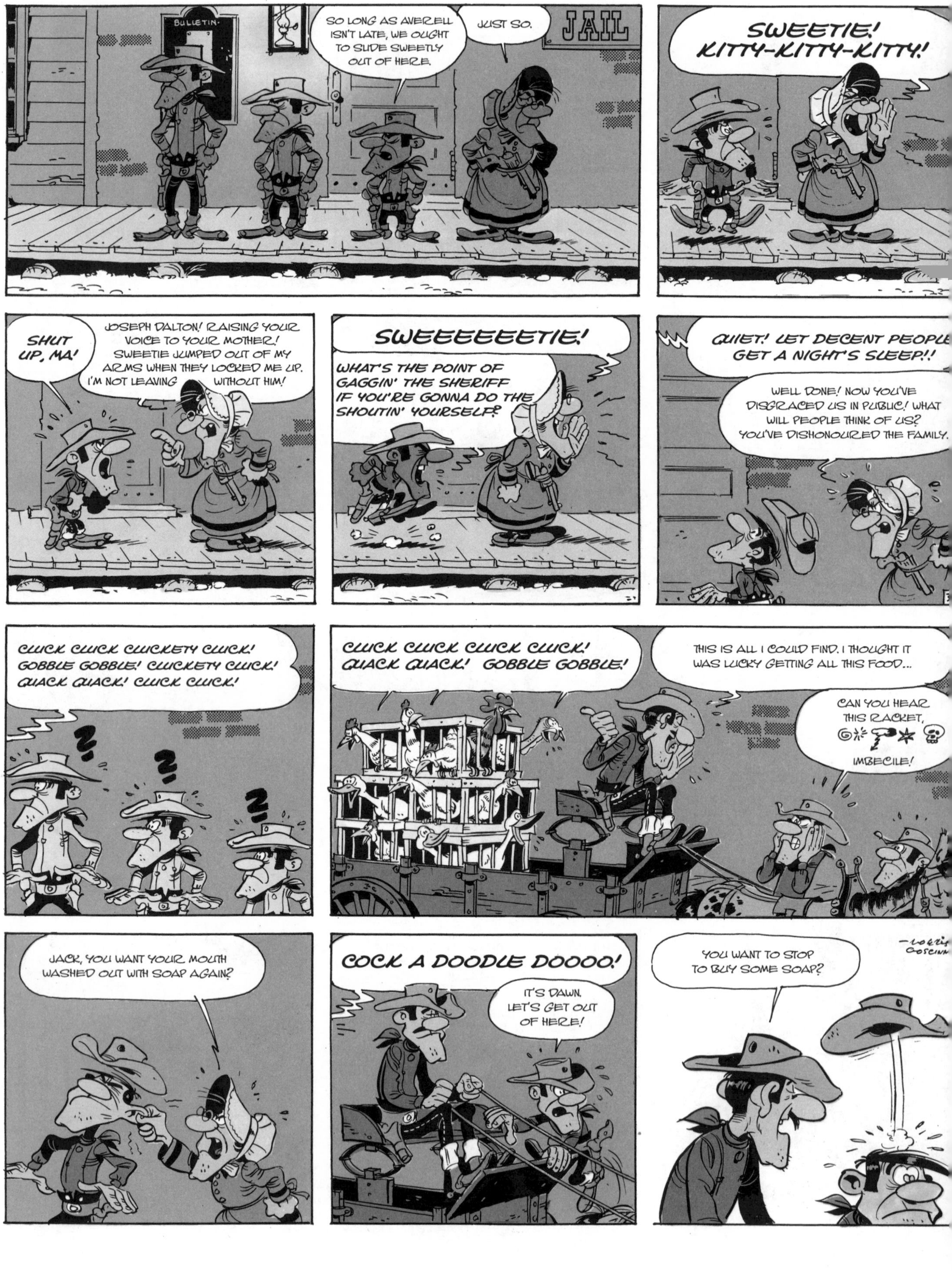
BULLETIN
JAIL
SO LONG AS AVERELL ISN'T LATE, WE OUGHT TO SLIDE SWEETLY OUT OF HERE.
JUST SO.
SWEETIE! KITTY-KITTY-KITTY!
SHUT UP, MA!
JOSEPH DALTON! RAISING YOUR VOICE TO YOUR MOTHER! SWEETIE JUMPED OUT OF MY ARMS WHEN THEY LOCKED ME UP. I'M NOT LEAVING WITHOUT HIM!
SWEEEEEEETIE!
WHAT'S THE POINT OF GAGGIN' THE SHERIFF IF YOU'RE GONNA DO THE SHOUTIN' YOURSELF?
QUIET! LET DECENT PEOPLE GET A NIGHT'S SLEEP!!
WELL DONE! NOW YOU'VE DISGRACED US IN PUBLIC! WHAT WILL PEOPLE THINK OF US? YOU'VE DISHONOURED THE FAMILY.
CLUCK CLUCK CLUCKETY CLUCK! GOBBLE GOBBLE! CLUCKETY CLUCK! QUACK QUACK! CLUCK CLUCK!
CLUCK CLUCK CLUCK CLUCK! QUACK QUACK! GOBBLE GOBBLE!
THIS IS ALL I COULD FIND. I THOUGHT IT WAS LUCKY GETTING ALL THIS FOOD...
CAN YOU HEAR THIS RACKET, IMBECILE!
JACK, YOU WANT YOUR MOUTH WASHED OUT WITH SOAP AGAIN?
COCK A DOODLE DOOOO!
IT'S DAWN. LET'S GET OUT OF HERE!
YOU WANT TO STOP TO BUY SOME SOAP?

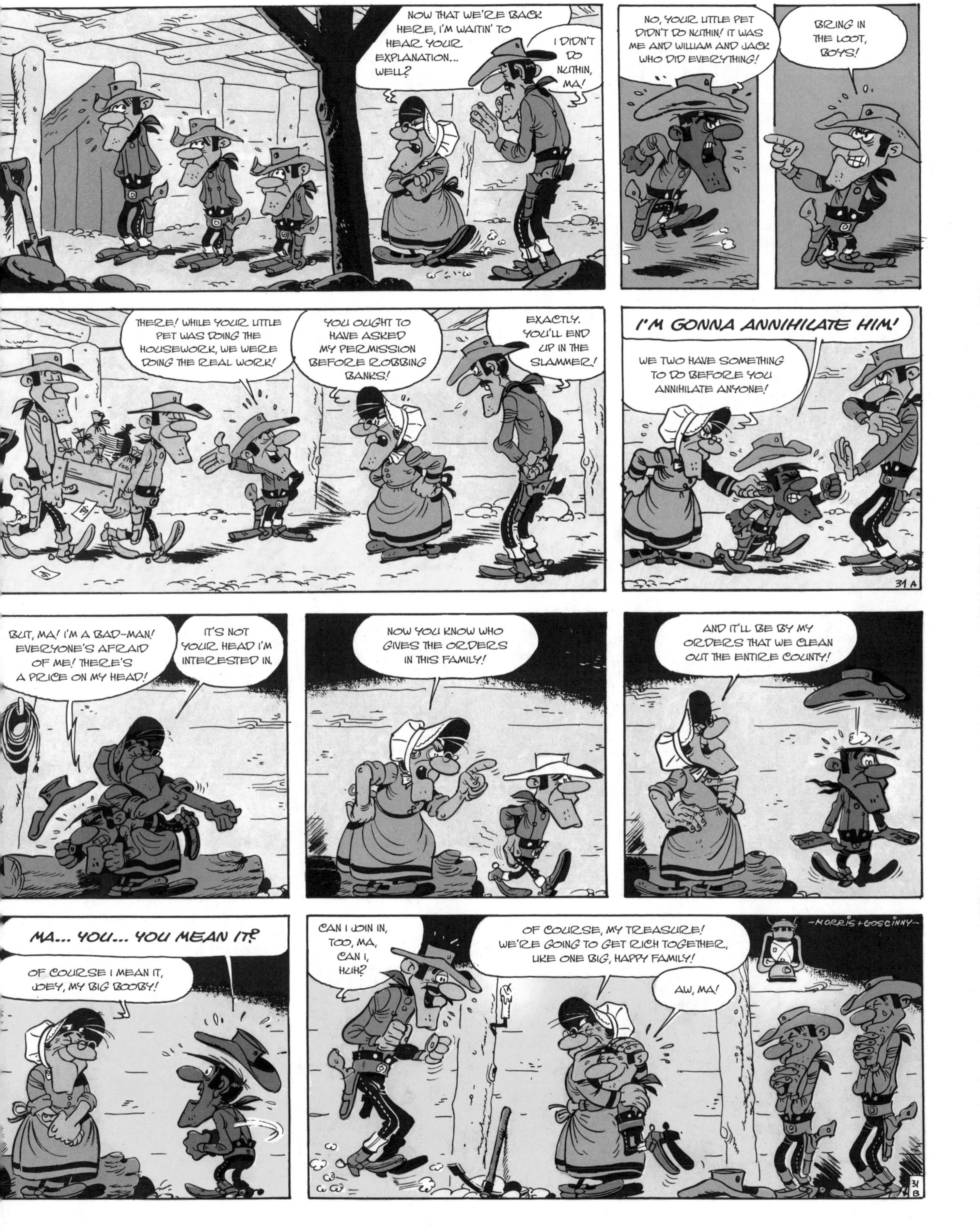
NOW THAT WE'RE BACK HERE, I'M WAITIN' TO HEAR YOUR EXPLANATION... WELL?
I DIDN'T DO NUTHIN, MA!
NO, YOUR LITTLE PET DIDN'T DO NUTHIN! IT WAS ME AND WILLIAM AND JACK WHO DID EVERYTHING!
BRING IN THE LOOT, BOYS!
THERE! WHILE YOUR LITTLE PET WAS DOING THE HOUSEWORK, WE WERE DOING THE REAL WORK!
YOU OUGHT TO HAVE ASKED MY PERMISSION BEFORE ROBBING BANKS!
EXACTLY. YOU'LL END UP IN THE SLAMMER!
I'M GONNA ANNIHILATE HIM!
WE TWO HAVE SOMETHING TO DO BEFORE YOU ANNIHILATE ANYONE!
31 A
BUT, MA! I'M A BAD-MAN! EVERYONE'S AFRAID OF ME! THERE'S A PRICE ON MY HEAD!
IT'S NOT YOUR HEAD I'M INTERESTED IN.
NOW YOU KNOW WHO GIVES THE ORDERS IN THIS FAMILY!
AND IT'LL BE BY MY ORDERS THAT WE CLEAN OUT THE ENTIRE COUNTY!
MA... YOU... YOU MEAN IT?
OF COURSE I MEAN IT, JOEY, MY BIG BOOBY!
-MORRIS+GOSCINNY-
CAN I JOIN IN, TOO, MA, CAN I, HUH?
OF COURSE, MY TREASURE! WE'RE GOING TO GET RICH TOGETHER, LIKE ONE BIG, HAPPY FAMILY!
AW, MA!
31 B

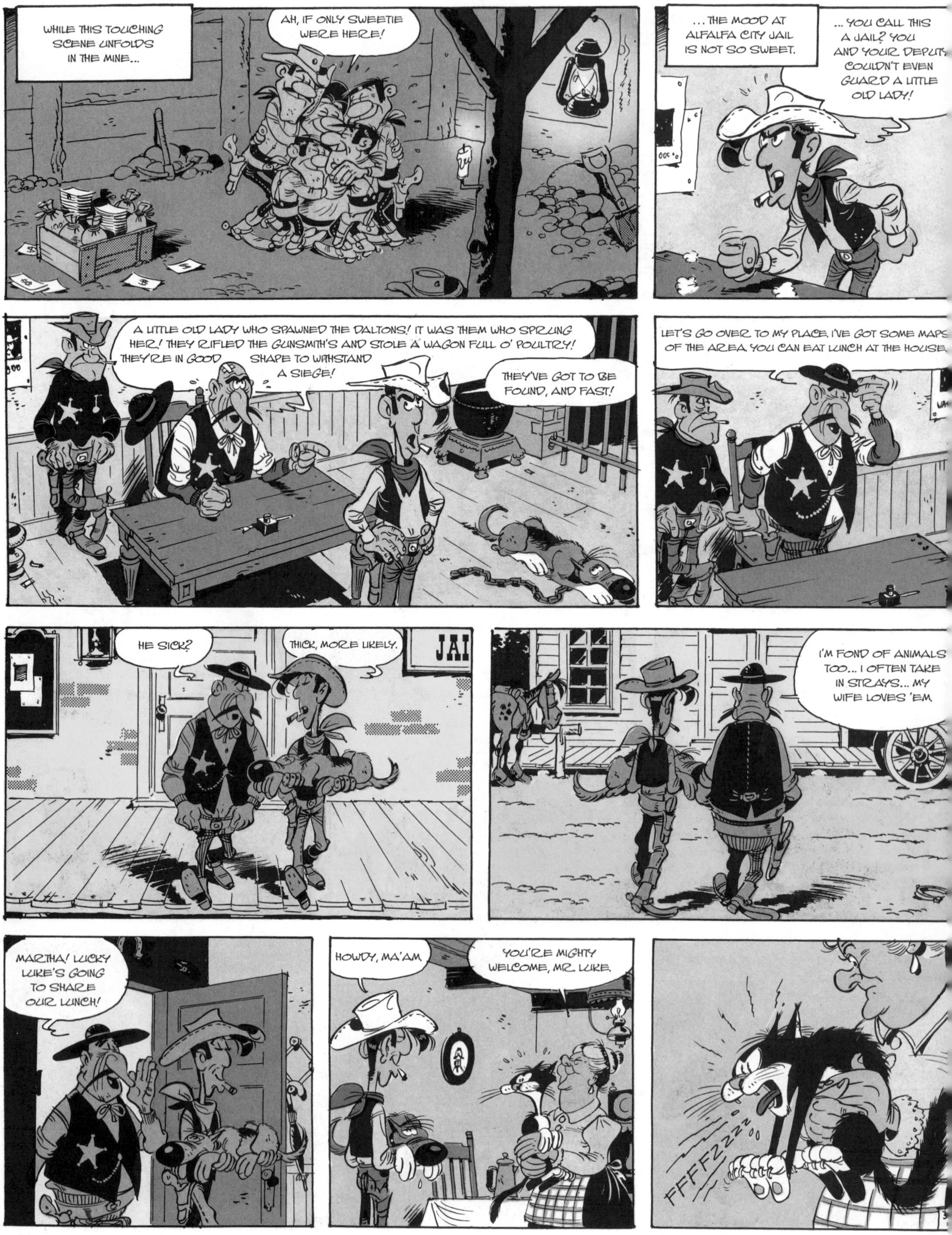

WHILE THIS TOUCHING SCENE UNFOLDS IN THE MINE...
AH, IF ONLY SWEETIE WERE HERE!
... THE MOOD AT ALFALFA CITY JAIL IS NOT SO SWEET.
... YOU CALL THIS A JAIL? YOU AND YOUR DEPUT COULDN'T EVEN GUARD A LITTLE OLD LADY!
A LITTLE OLD LADY WHO SPAWNED THE DALTONS! IT WAS THEM WHO SPRUNG HER! THEY RIFLED THE GUNSMITH'S AND STOLE A WAGON FULL O' POULTRY! THEY'RE IN GOOD SHAPE TO WITHSTAND A SIEGE!
THEY'VE GOT TO BE FOUND, AND FAST!
LET'S GO OVER TO MY PLACE. I'VE GOT SOME MAPS OF THE AREA. YOU CAN EAT LUNCH AT THE HOUSE.
HE SICK?
THICK, MORE LIKELY.
JAI
I'M FOND OF ANIMALS TOO... I OFTEN TAKE IN STRAYS... MY WIFE LOVES 'EM.
MARTHA! LUCKY LUKE'S GOING TO SHARE OUR LUNCH!
HOWDY, MA'AM.
YOU'RE MIGHTY WELCOME, MR LUKE.
FFFFZZZZ

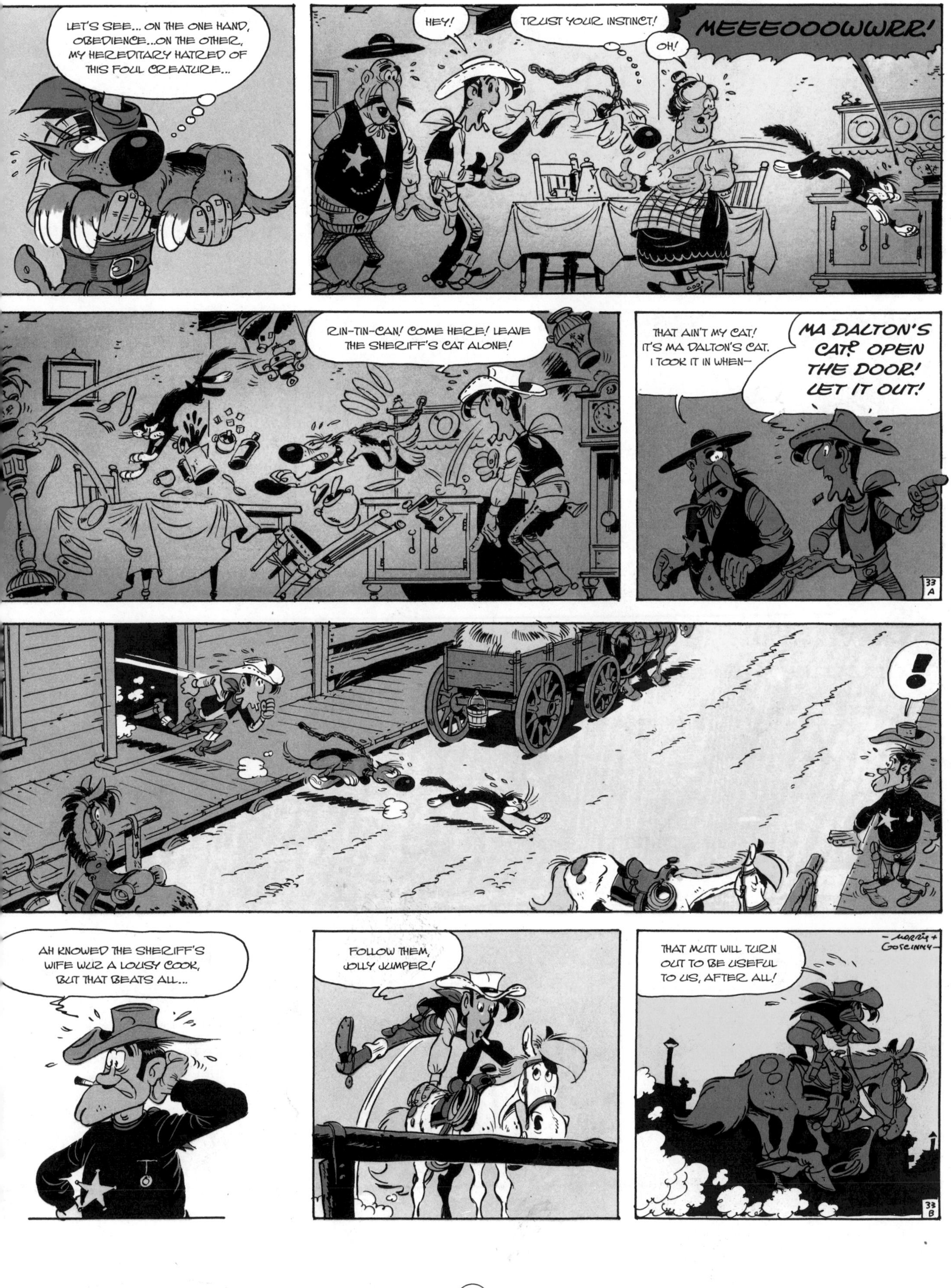
LET'S SEE... ON THE ONE HAND, OBEDIENCE...ON THE OTHER, MY HEREDITARY HATRED OF THIS FOUL CREATURE...
HEY!
TRUST YOUR INSTINCT!
OH!
MEEEOOOWWRR!
RIN-TIN-CAN! COME HERE! LEAVE THE SHERIFF'S CAT ALONE!
THAT AIN'T MY CAT! IT'S MA DALTON'S CAT. I TOOK IT IN WHEN—
MA DALTON'S CAT? OPEN THE DOOR! LET IT OUT!
33 A
!
AH KNOWED THE SHERIFF'S WIFE WUZ A LOUSY COOK, BUT THAT BEATS ALL...
FOLLOW THEM, JOLLY JUMPER!
—MORRIS + GOSCINNY—
THAT MUTT WILL TURN OUT TO BE USEFUL TO US, AFTER ALL!
33 B

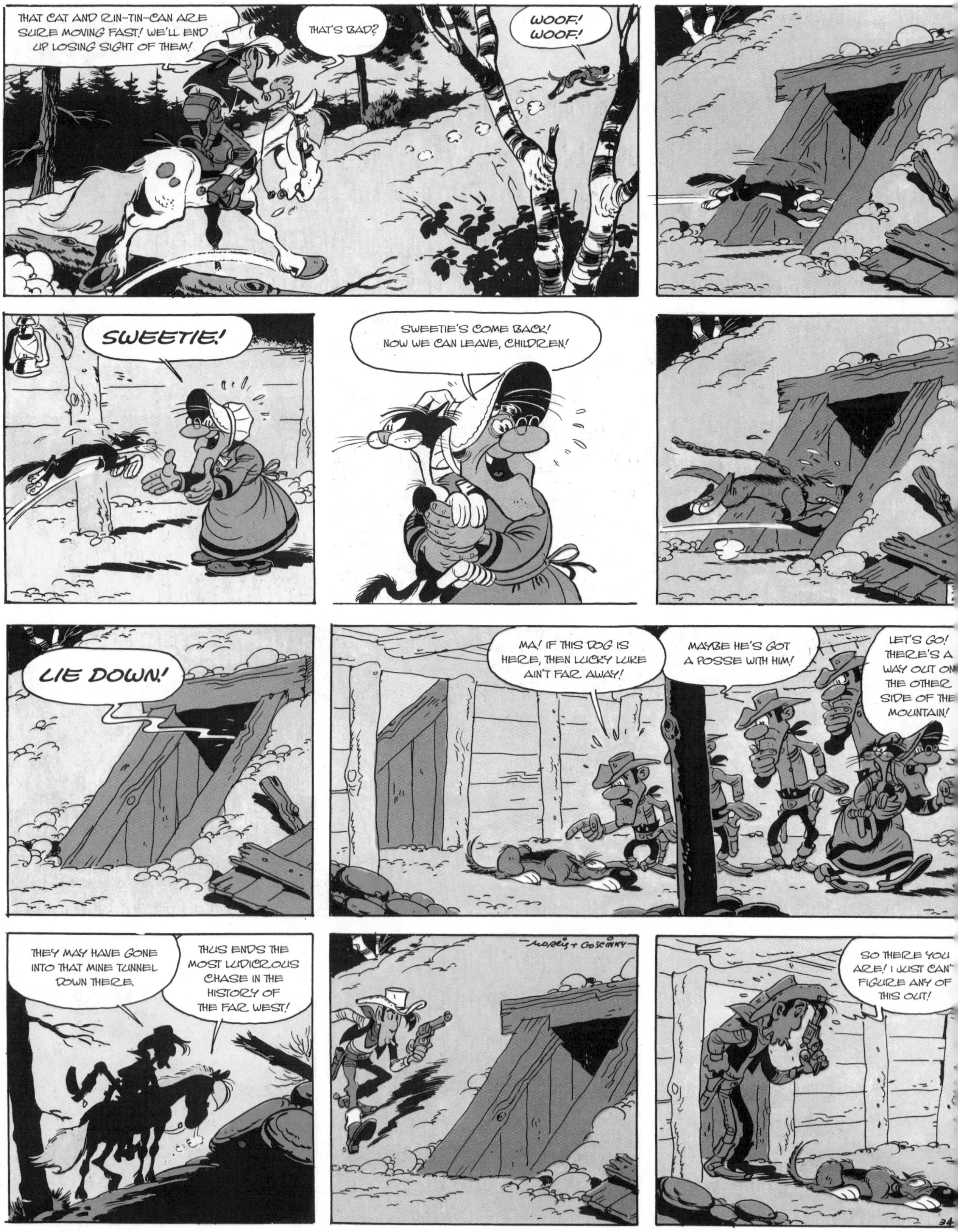

THAT CAT AND RIN-TIN-CAN ARE SURE MOVING FAST! WE'LL END UP LOSING SIGHT OF THEM!
THAT'S BAD?
WOOF! WOOF!
SWEETIE!
SWEETIE'S COME BACK! NOW WE CAN LEAVE, CHILDREN!
LIE DOWN!
MA! IF THIS DOG IS HERE, THEN LUCKY LUKE AIN'T FAR AWAY!
MAYBE HE'S GOT A POSSE WITH HIM!
LET'S GO! THERE'S A WAY OUT O THE OTHER SIDE OF THE MOUNTAIN!
THEY MAY HAVE GONE INTO THAT MINE TUNNEL DOWN THERE.
THUS ENDS THE MOST LUDICROUS CHASE IN THE HISTORY OF THE FAR WEST!
SO THERE YOU ARE! I JUST CAN' FIGURE ANY OF THIS OUT!

? · LET'S HEAD BACK TO CACTUS JUNCTION, JOLLY JUMPER. I RECKON WE'LL BE HEARING ABOUT THE DALTON FAMILY IN THESE PARTS...

AND INDEED, AT THE BANK IN SWEETBREAD PUEBLO... · IF IT ISN'T MA DALTON! · OPEN YOUR SAFE, COYOTE!

AT THE BANK OF LIMABEANVILLE... · MY SAFE? BUT, MA DALTON... · YEAH! YOUR SAFE!

AND SIMULTANEOUSLY IN THE BANK OF MATTRESS SPRINGS... · HERE, MA DALTON, HERE YOU ARE! · 1000

AND OVER ON THE OTHER SIDE OF THE COUNTY IN THE BANK OF LETTUCE FALLS. · ULP! MA DALTON! THIS IS UNUSUAL, EVEN FOR YOU!

35 A

BUT... ?! IDIOT! YOU SHOULD BE ROBBING A DIFFERENT BANK TODAY! · I BEG YOUR PARDON! MA DID ALL THE PLANNING. IT IS I WHO DOES THE JOB HERE TODAY! · COME QUICK! THE BOSS HAS BEEN TAKEN ILL!

The Cactus Junction
CLARION

MA DALTON'S REIGN OF TERROR

Seen Everywhere at the Same Time

POLICE BAFFLED

Twelve Banks Robbed

He ear nes lus phy pho- and rough ig and ignition gadfly from ow con- unleash- ng about

The town settled down to everyone glad that there

The sheriff was too late to prevent a mob from hauling Badman off to the edge of

FEAR SPREADS AMONG THE CITIZENS... · ...AND WATCH OUT FOR LITTLE OLD LADIES, BETTY!

AND SOMEWHERE IN THE HILLS... · YOU CAN COUNT THE LOOT LATER, CHILDREN, LET'S EAT!

MORRIS + GOSCINNY

35 B

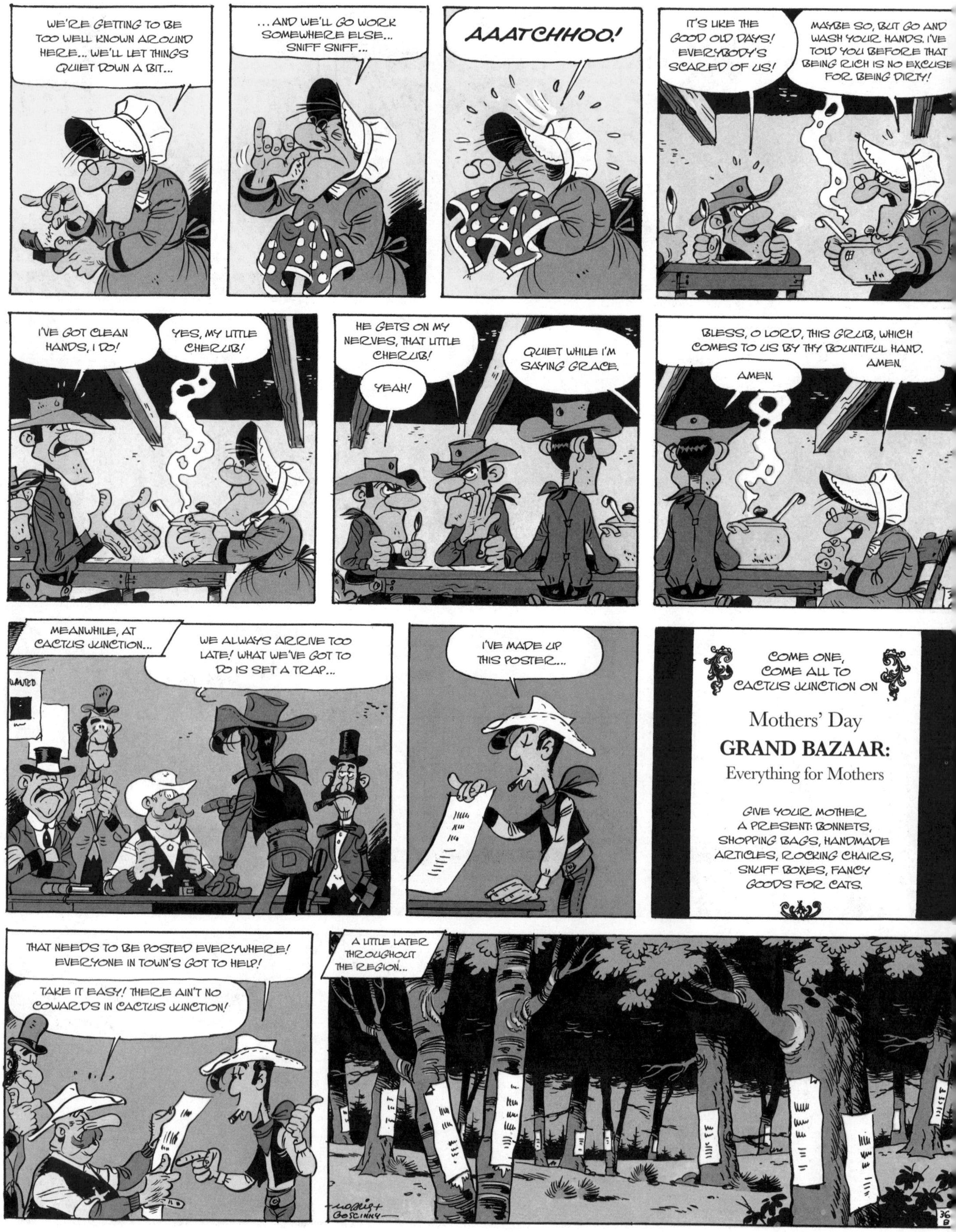

WE'RE GETTING TO BE TOO WELL KNOWN AROUND HERE... WE'LL LET THINGS QUIET DOWN A BIT...
...AND WE'LL GO WORK SOMEWHERE ELSE... SNIFF SNIFF...
AAATCHHOO!
IT'S LIKE THE GOOD OLD DAYS! EVERYBODY'S SCARED OF US!
MAYBE SO, BUT GO AND WASH YOUR HANDS. I'VE TOLD YOU BEFORE THAT BEING RICH IS NO EXCUSE FOR BEING DIRTY!
I'VE GOT CLEAN HANDS, I DO!
YES, MY LITTLE CHERUB!
HE GETS ON MY NERVES, THAT LITTLE CHERUB!
YEAH!
QUIET WHILE I'M SAYING GRACE.
BLESS, O LORD, THIS GRUB, WHICH COMES TO US BY THY BOUNTIFUL HAND.
AMEN.
AMEN.
MEANWHILE, AT CACTUS JUNCTION...
WE ALWAYS ARRIVE TOO LATE! WHAT WE'VE GOT TO DO IS SET A TRAP...
I'VE MADE UP THIS POSTER...
COME ONE, COME ALL TO CACTUS JUNCTION ON
Mothers' Day
GRAND BAZAAR:
Everything for Mothers
GIVE YOUR MOTHER A PRESENT: BONNETS, SHOPPING BAGS, HANDMADE ARTICLES, ROCKING CHAIRS, SNUFF BOXES, FANCY GOODS FOR CATS.
THAT NEEDS TO BE POSTED EVERYWHERE! EVERYONE IN TOWN'S GOT TO HELP!
TAKE IT EASY! THERE AIN'T NO COWARDS IN CACTUS JUNCTION!
A LITTLE LATER THROUGHOUT THE REGION...

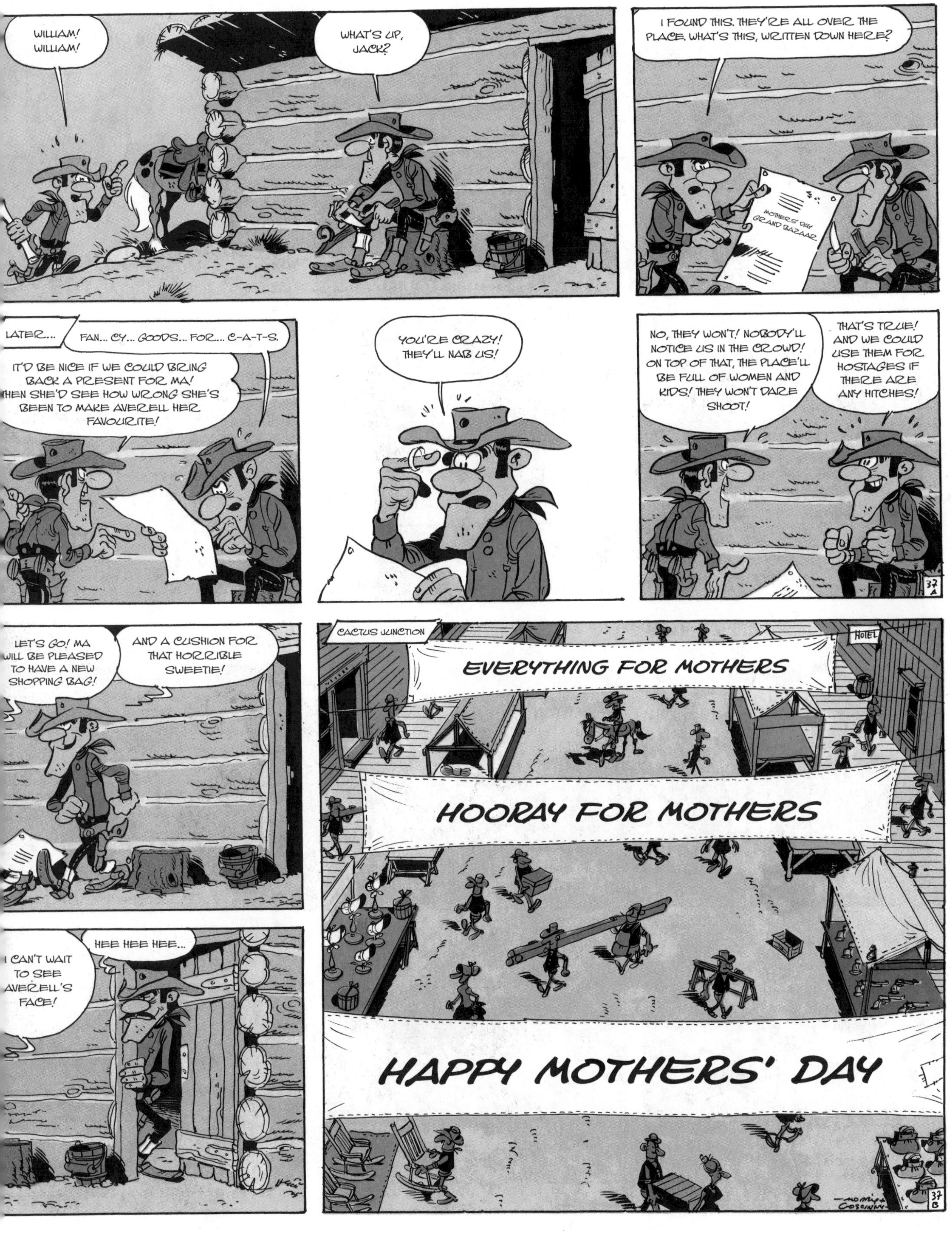
WILLIAM! WILLIAM!
WHAT'S UP, JACK?
I FOUND THIS. THEY'RE ALL OVER THE PLACE. WHAT'S THIS, WRITTEN DOWN HERE?
MOTHERS' DAY GRAND BAZAAR
LATER...
FAN... CY... GOODS... FOR... C-A-T-S.
IT'D BE NICE IF WE COULD BRING BACK A PRESENT FOR MA! THEN SHE'D SEE HOW WRONG SHE'S BEEN TO MAKE AVERELL HER FAVOURITE!
YOU'RE CRAZY! THEY'LL NAB US!
NO, THEY WON'T! NOBODY'LL NOTICE US IN THE CROWD! ON TOP OF THAT, THE PLACE'LL BE FULL OF WOMEN AND KIDS! THEY WON'T DARE SHOOT!
THAT'S TRUE! AND WE COULD USE THEM FOR HOSTAGES IF THERE ARE ANY HITCHES!
37 A
LET'S GO! MA WILL BE PLEASED TO HAVE A NEW SHOPPING BAG!
AND A CUSHION FOR THAT HORRIBLE SWEETIE!
I CAN'T WAIT TO SEE AVERELL'S FACE!
HEE HEE HEE...
CACTUS JUNCTION
HOTEL
EVERYTHING FOR MOTHERS
HOORAY FOR MOTHERS
HAPPY MOTHERS' DAY
37 B

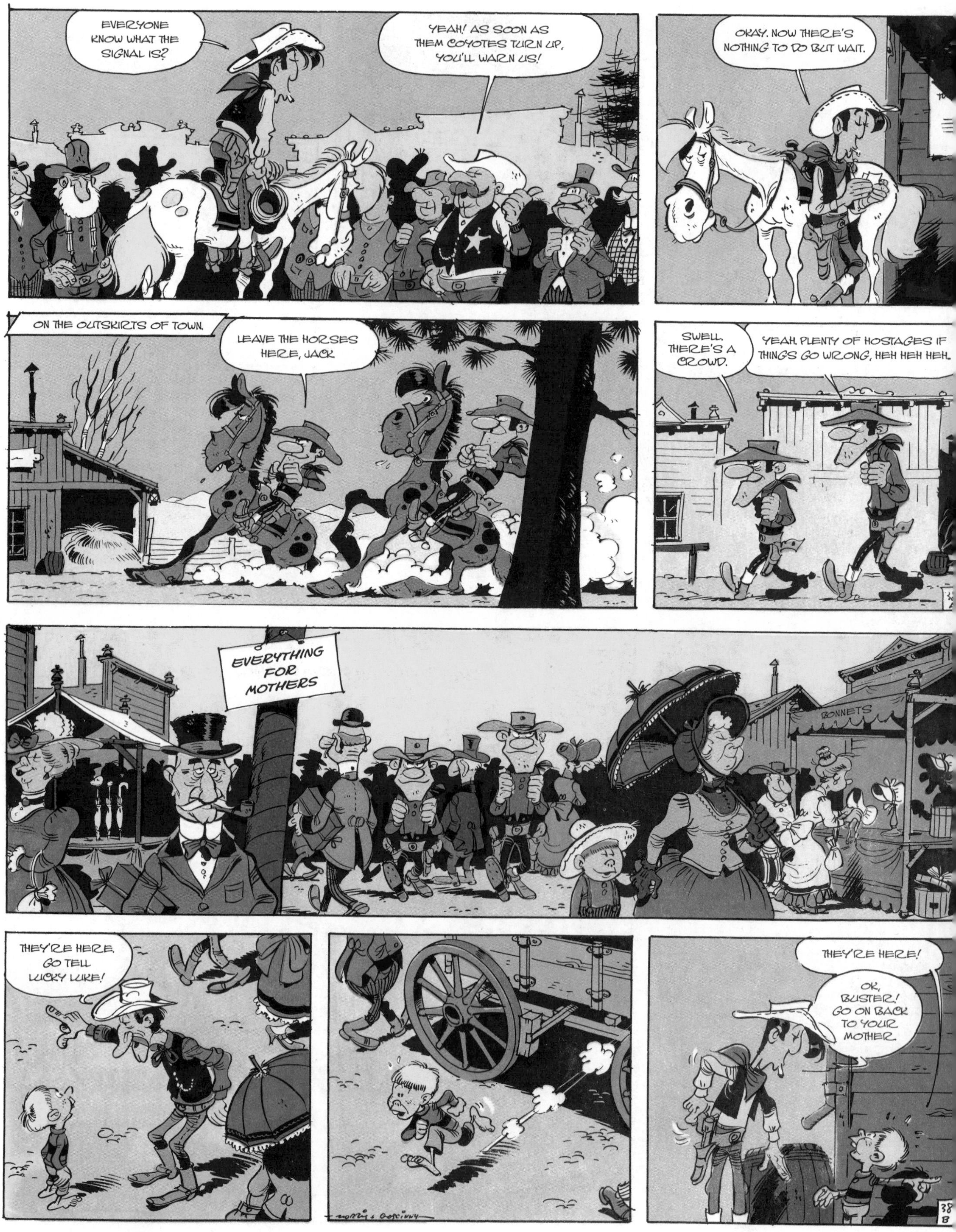
EVERYONE KNOW WHAT THE SIGNAL IS?
YEAH! AS SOON AS THEM COYOTES TURN UP, YOU'LL WARN US!
OKAY. NOW THERE'S NOTHING TO DO BUT WAIT.
ON THE OUTSKIRTS OF TOWN.
LEAVE THE HORSES HERE, JACK
SWELL. THERE'S A CROWD.
YEAH. PLENTY OF HOSTAGES IF THINGS GO WRONG, HEH HEH HEH.
EVERYTHING FOR MOTHERS
BONNETS
THEY'RE HERE. GO TELL LUCKY LUKE!
THEY'RE HERE!
OK, BUSTER! GO ON BACK TO YOUR MOTHER
38 B

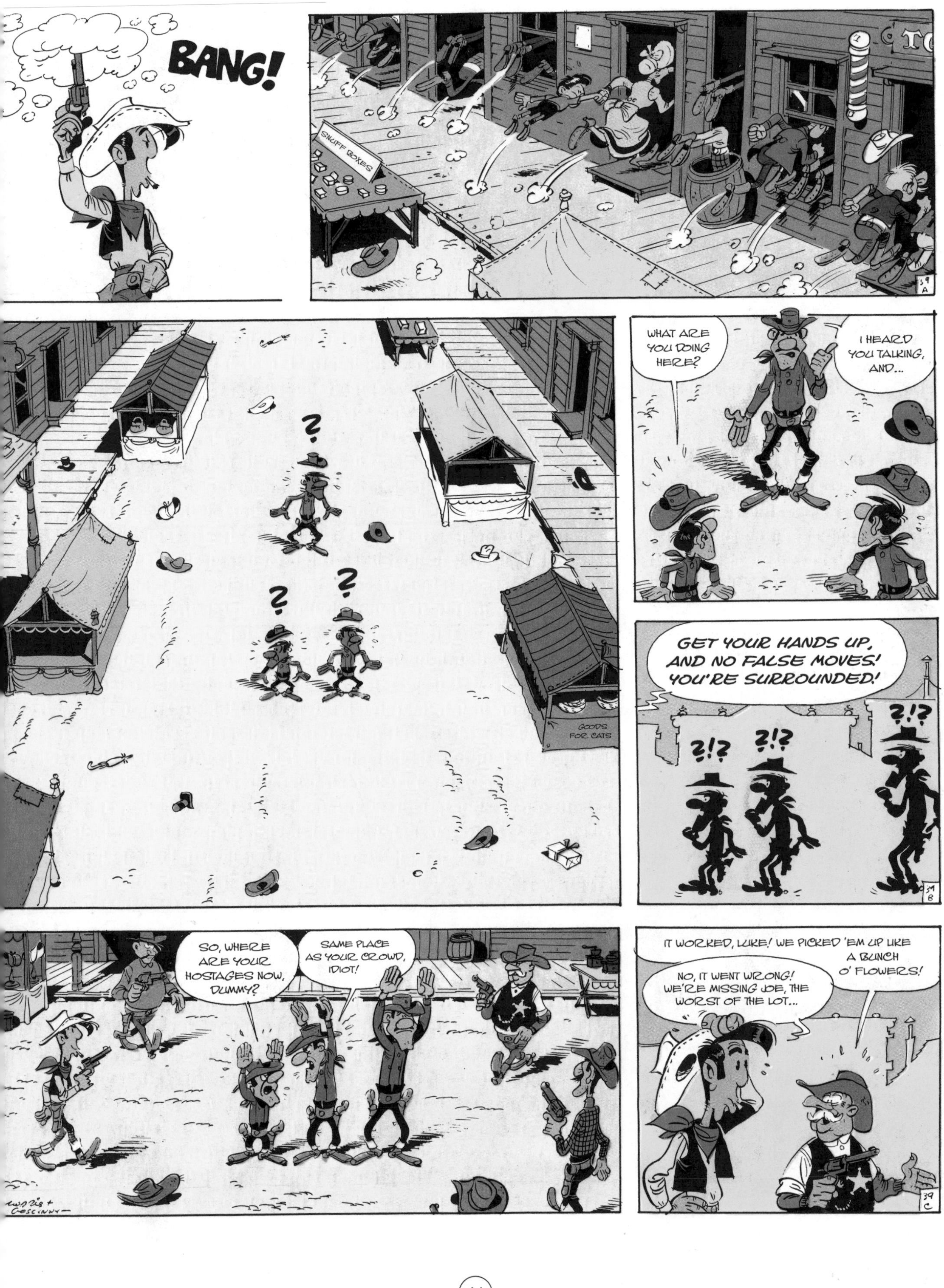
BANG!
SNUFF BOXES
GOODS FOR CATS
WHAT ARE YOU DOING HERE?
I HEARD YOU TALKING, AND...
GET YOUR HANDS UP, AND NO FALSE MOVES! YOU'RE SURROUNDED!
?!?
?!?
?!?
SO, WHERE ARE YOUR HOSTAGES NOW, DUMMY?
SAME PLACE AS YOUR CROWD, IDIOT!
IT WORKED, LUKE! WE PICKED 'EM UP LIKE A BUNCH O' FLOWERS!
NO, IT WENT WRONG! WE'RE MISSING JOE, THE WORST OF THE LOT...

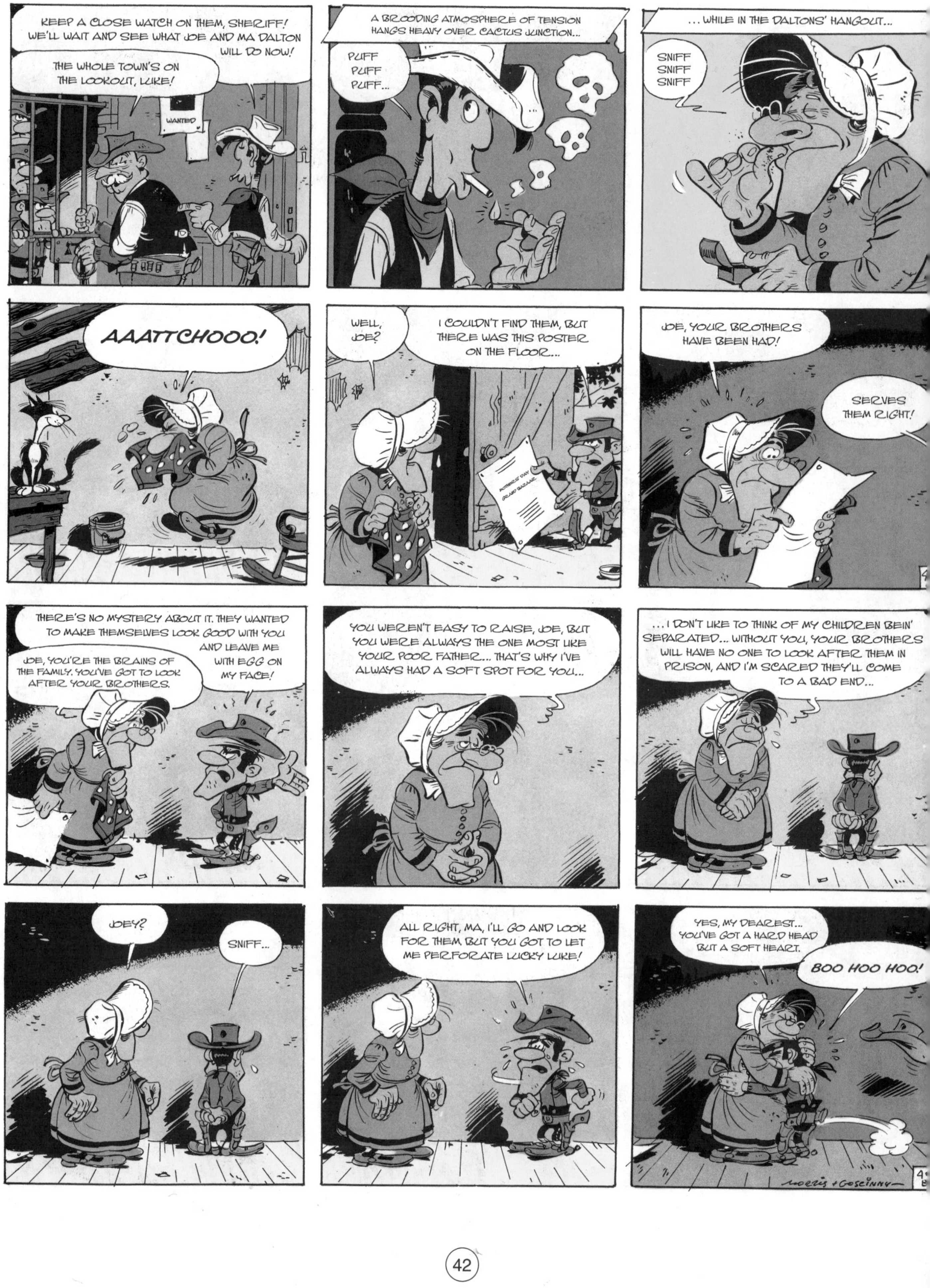
KEEP A CLOSE WATCH ON THEM, SHERIFF! WE'LL WAIT AND SEE WHAT JOE AND MA DALTON WILL DO NOW!
THE WHOLE TOWN'S ON THE LOOKOUT, LUKE!
WANTED
A BROODING ATMOSPHERE OF TENSION HANGS HEAVY OVER CACTUS JUNCTION...
PUFF PUFF PUFF...
... WHILE IN THE DALTONS' HANGOUT...
SNIFF SNIFF SNIFF
AAATTCHOOO!
WELL, JOE?
I COULDN'T FIND THEM, BUT THERE WAS THIS POSTER ON THE FLOOR...
JOE, YOUR BROTHERS HAVE BEEN HAD!
SERVES THEM RIGHT!
THERE'S NO MYSTERY ABOUT IT. THEY WANTED TO MAKE THEMSELVES LOOK GOOD WITH YOU AND LEAVE ME WITH EGG ON MY FACE!
JOE, YOU'RE THE BRAINS OF THE FAMILY. YOU'VE GOT TO LOOK AFTER YOUR BROTHERS.
YOU WEREN'T EASY TO RAISE, JOE, BUT YOU WERE ALWAYS THE ONE MOST LIKE YOUR POOR FATHER... THAT'S WHY I'VE ALWAYS HAD A SOFT SPOT FOR YOU...
... I DON'T LIKE TO THINK OF MY CHILDREN BEIN' SEPARATED... WITHOUT YOU, YOUR BROTHERS WILL HAVE NO ONE TO LOOK AFTER THEM IN PRISON, AND I'M SCARED THEY'LL COME TO A BAD END...
JOEY?
SNIFF...
ALL RIGHT, MA, I'LL GO AND LOOK FOR THEM BUT YOU GOT TO LET ME PERFORATE LUCKY LUKE!
YES, MY DEAREST... YOU'VE GOT A HARD HEAD BUT A SOFT HEART.
BOO HOO HOO!

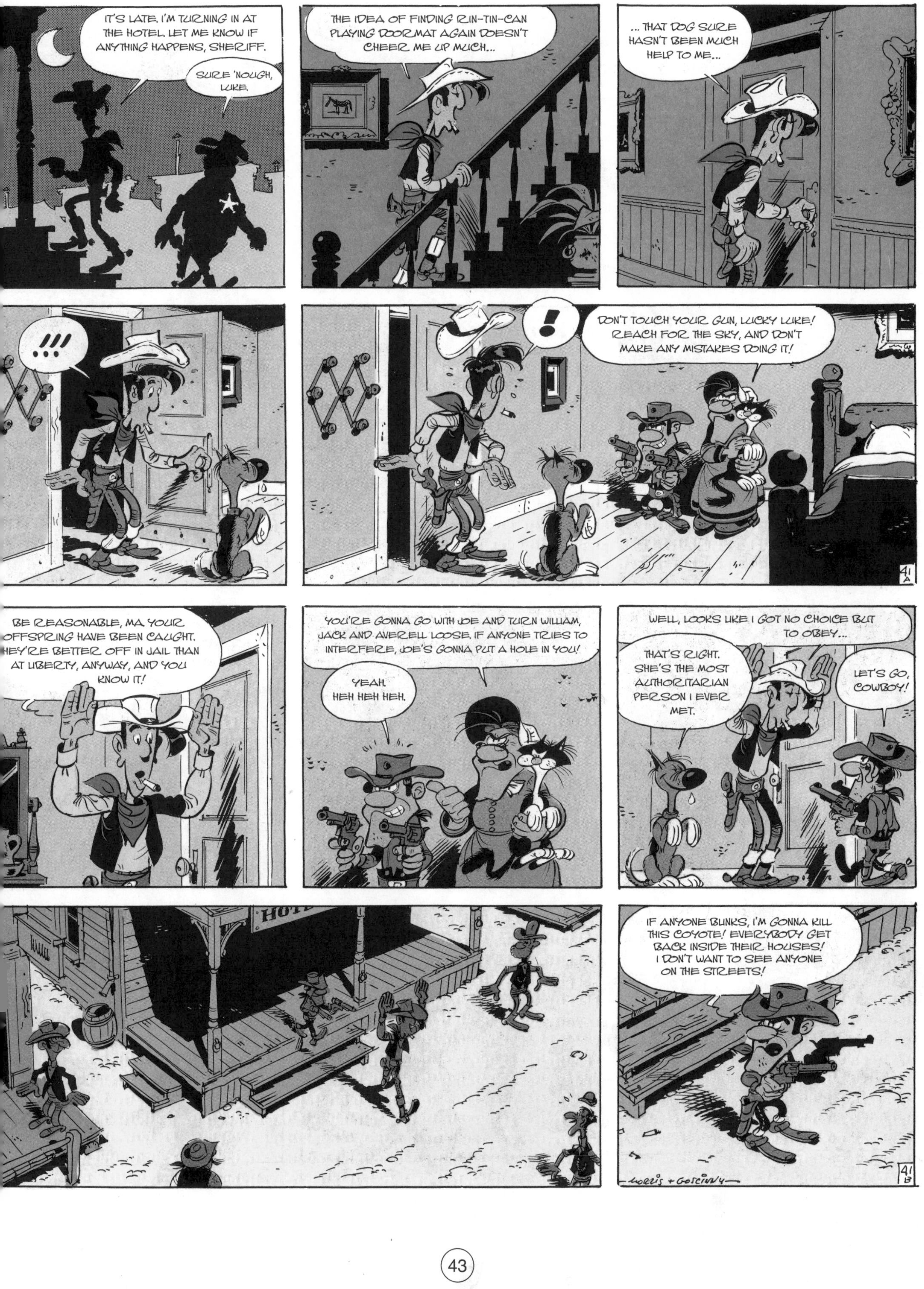
IT'S LATE. I'M TURNING IN AT THE HOTEL. LET ME KNOW IF ANYTHING HAPPENS, SHERIFF.
SURE 'NOUGH, LUKE.
THE IDEA OF FINDING RIN-TIN-CAN PLAYING DOORMAT AGAIN DOESN'T CHEER ME UP MUCH...
... THAT DOG SURE HASN'T BEEN MUCH HELP TO ME...
!!!
!
DON'T TOUCH YOUR GUN, LUCKY LUKE! REACH FOR THE SKY, AND DON'T MAKE ANY MISTAKES DOING IT!
BE REASONABLE, MA. YOUR OFFSPRING HAVE BEEN CAUGHT. HEY'RE BETTER OFF IN JAIL THAN AT LIBERTY, ANYWAY, AND YOU KNOW IT!
YOU'RE GONNA GO WITH JOE AND TURN WILLIAM, JACK AND AVERELL LOOSE. IF ANYONE TRIES TO INTERFERE, JOE'S GONNA PUT A HOLE IN YOU!
YEAH. HEH HEH HEH.
WELL, LOOKS LIKE I GOT NO CHOICE BUT TO OBEY...
THAT'S RIGHT. SHE'S THE MOST AUTHORITARIAN PERSON I EVER MET.
LET'S GO, COWBOY!
IF ANYONE BLINKS, I'M GONNA KILL THIS COYOTE! EVERYBODY GET BACK INSIDE THEIR HOUSES! I DON'T WANT TO SEE ANYONE ON THE STREETS!
MORRIS + GOSCINNY

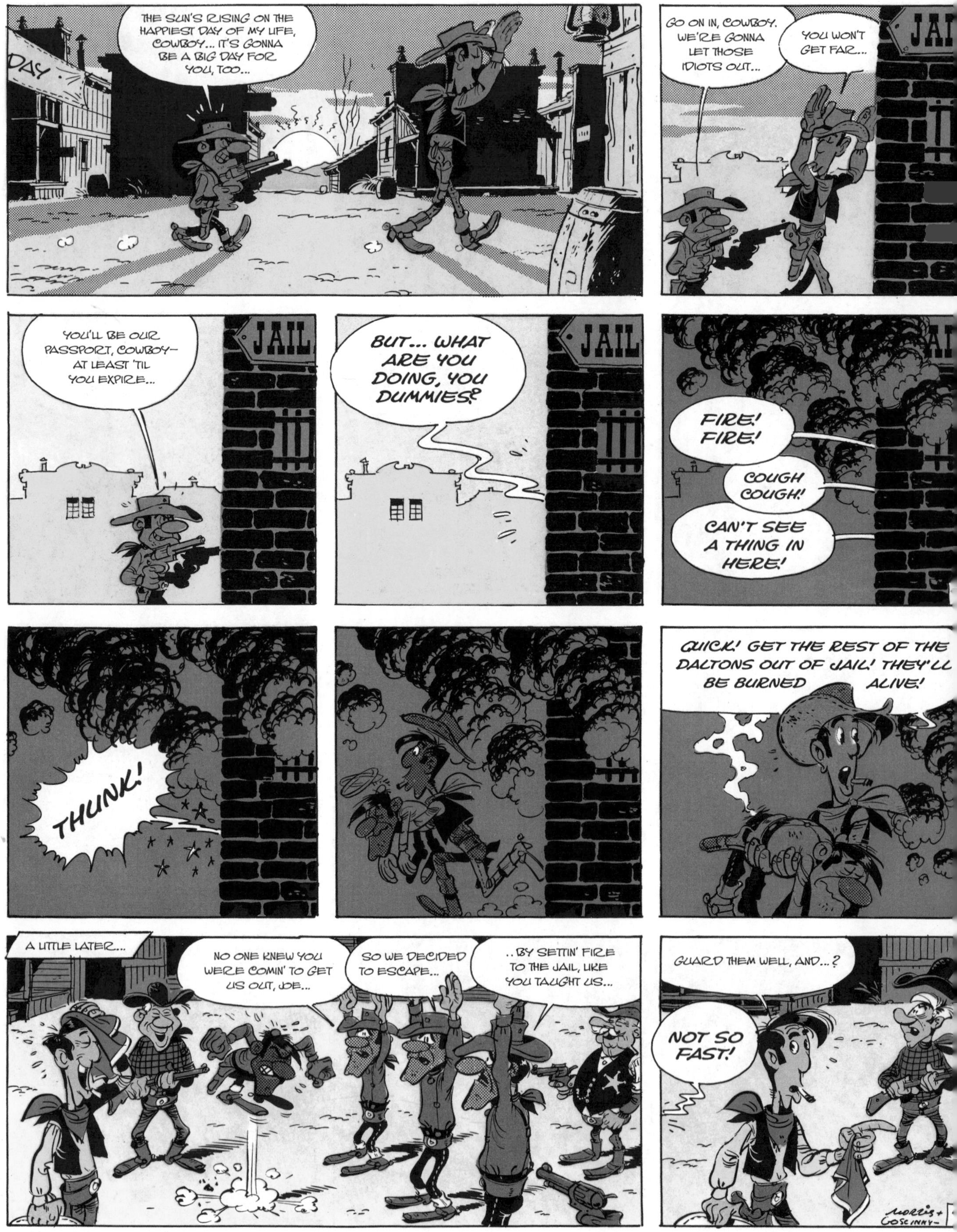

THE SUN'S RISING ON THE HAPPIEST DAY OF MY LIFE, COWBOY... IT'S GONNA BE A BIG DAY FOR YOU, TOO...
GO ON IN, COWBOY. WE'RE GONNA LET THOSE IDIOTS OUT...
YOU WON'T GET FAR...
YOU'LL BE OUR PASSPORT, COWBOY– AT LEAST 'TIL YOU EXPIRE...
BUT... WHAT ARE YOU DOING, YOU DUMMIES?
FIRE! FIRE!
COUGH COUGH!
CAN'T SEE A THING IN HERE!
THUNK!
QUICK! GET THE REST OF THE DALTONS OUT OF JAIL! THEY'LL BE BURNED ALIVE!
A LITTLE LATER...
NO ONE KNEW YOU WERE COMIN' TO GET US OUT, JOE...
SO WE DECIDED TO ESCAPE...
..BY SETTIN' FIRE TO THE JAIL, LIKE YOU TAUGHT US...
GUARD THEM WELL, AND...?
NOT SO FAST!

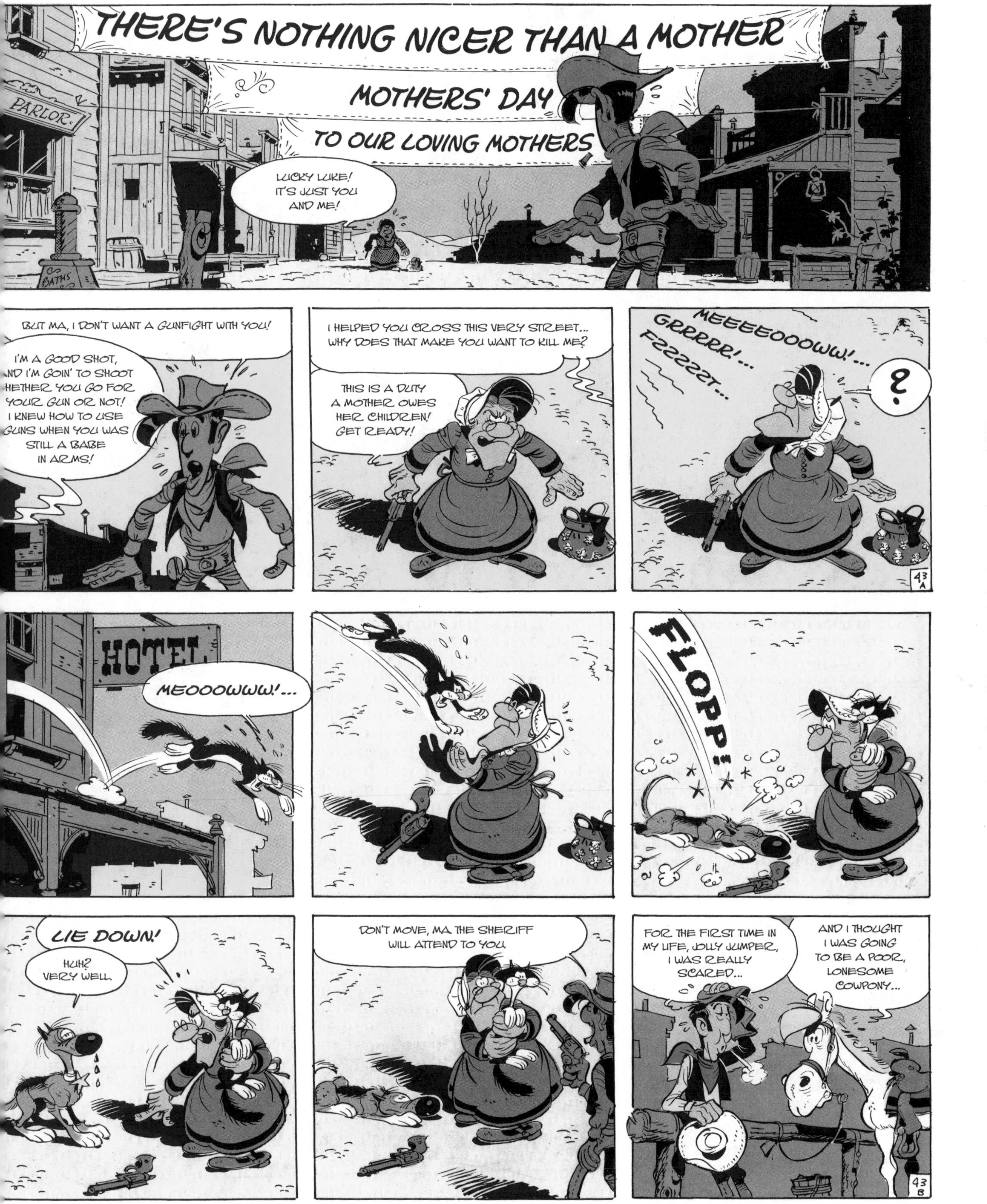

THERE'S NOTHING NICER THAN A MOTHER
MOTHERS' DAY
TO OUR LOVING MOTHERS
PARLOR
LUCKY LUKE! IT'S JUST YOU AND ME!
BATHS
BUT MA, I DON'T WANT A GUNFIGHT WITH YOU!
I'M A GOOD SHOT, AND I'M GOIN' TO SHOOT WHETHER YOU GO FOR YOUR GUN OR NOT! I KNEW HOW TO USE GUNS WHEN YOU WAS STILL A BABE IN ARMS!
I HELPED YOU CROSS THIS VERY STREET... WHY DOES THAT MAKE YOU WANT TO KILL ME?
THIS IS A DUTY A MOTHER OWES HER CHILDREN! GET READY!
MEEEEOOOOWW!...
GRRRRR!...
FZZZZZT...
?
HOTEL
MEOOOWWW!...
FLOPP!
LIE DOWN!
HUH? VERY WELL.
DON'T MOVE, MA THE SHERIFF WILL ATTEND TO YOU
FOR THE FIRST TIME IN MY LIFE, JOLLY JUMPER, I WAS REALLY SCARED...
AND I THOUGHT I WAS GOING TO BE A POOR, LONESOME COWPONY...

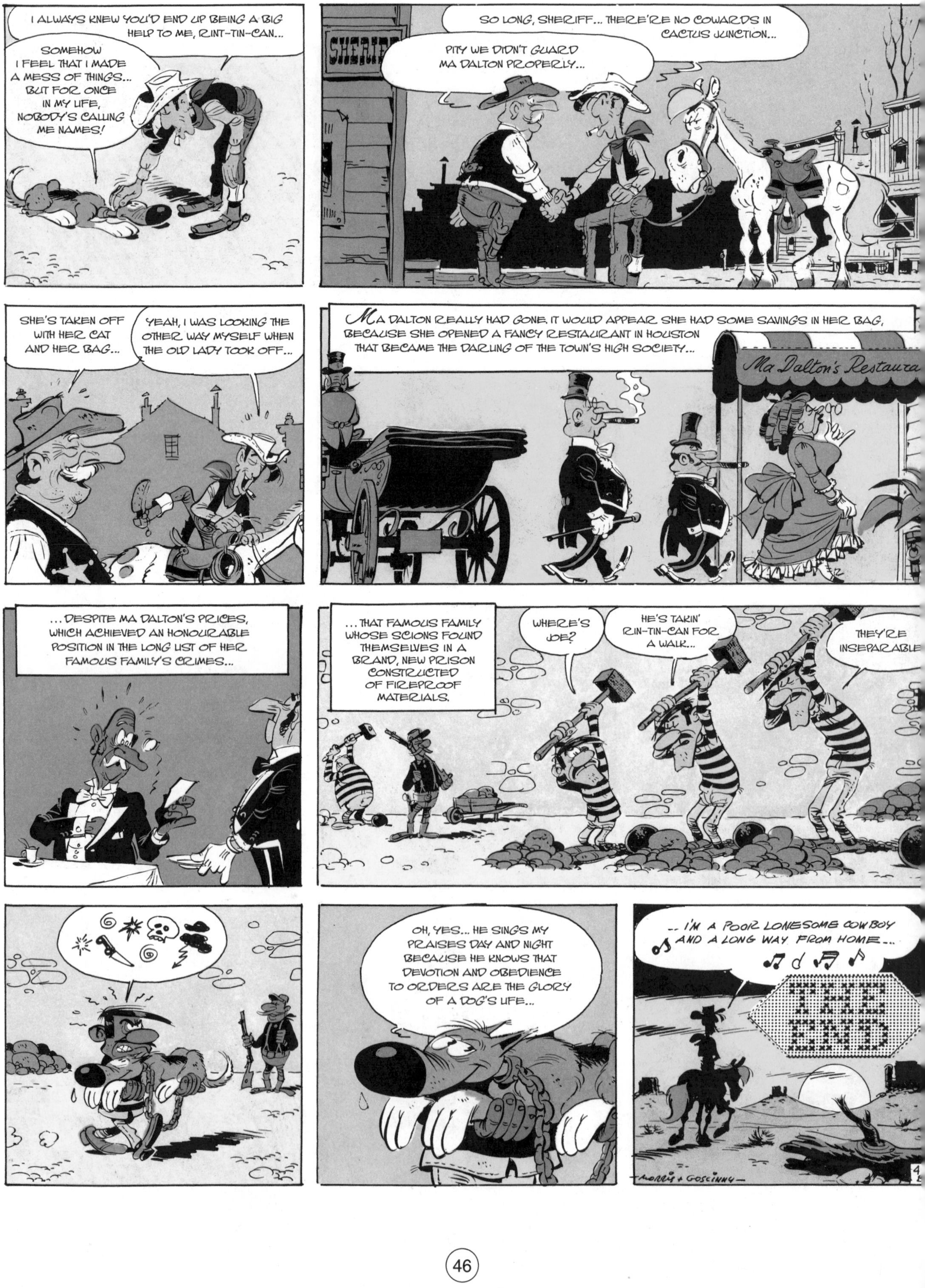
I ALWAYS KNEW YOU'D END UP BEING A BIG HELP TO ME, RINT-TIN-CAN...
SOMEHOW I FEEL THAT I MADE A MESS OF THINGS... BUT FOR ONCE IN MY LIFE, NOBODY'S CALLING ME NAMES!
SHERIF
SO LONG, SHERIFF... THERE'RE NO COWARDS IN CACTUS JUNCTION...
PITY WE DIDN'T GUARD MA DALTON PROPERLY...
SHE'S TAKEN OFF WITH HER CAT AND HER BAG...
YEAH, I WAS LOOKING THE OTHER WAY MYSELF WHEN THE OLD LADY TOOK OFF...
MA DALTON REALLY HAD GONE. IT WOULD APPEAR SHE HAD SOME SAVINGS IN HER BAG, BECAUSE SHE OPENED A FANCY RESTAURANT IN HOUSTON THAT BECAME THE DARLING OF THE TOWN'S HIGH SOCIETY...
Ma Dalton's Restaura
... DESPITE MA DALTON'S PRICES, WHICH ACHIEVED AN HONOURABLE POSITION IN THE LONG LIST OF HER FAMOUS FAMILY'S CRIMES...
... THAT FAMOUS FAMILY WHOSE SCIONS FOUND THEMSELVES IN A BRAND, NEW PRISON CONSTRUCTED OF FIREPROOF MATERIALS.
WHERE'S JOE?
HE'S TAKIN' RIN-TIN-CAN FOR A WALK...
THEY'RE INSEPARABLE
OH, YES... HE SINGS MY PRAISES DAY AND NIGHT BECAUSE HE KNOWS THAT DEVOTION AND OBEDIENCE TO ORDERS ARE THE GLORY OF A DOG'S LIFE...
.. I'M A POOR LONESOME COWBOY AND A LONG WAY FROM HOME...
THE END
MORRIS + GOSCINNY

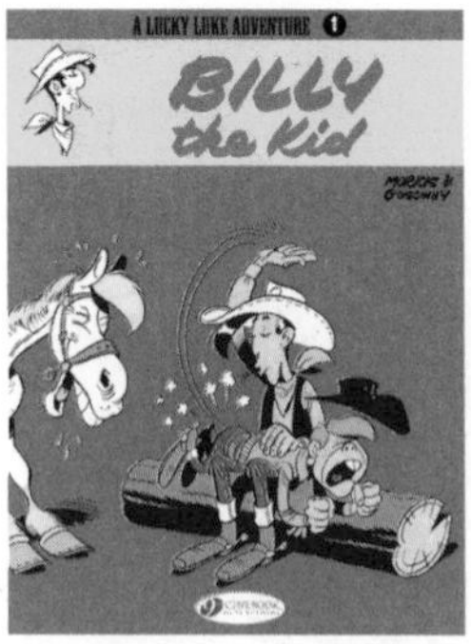
A LUCKY LUKE ADVENTURE 1
BILLY the Kid
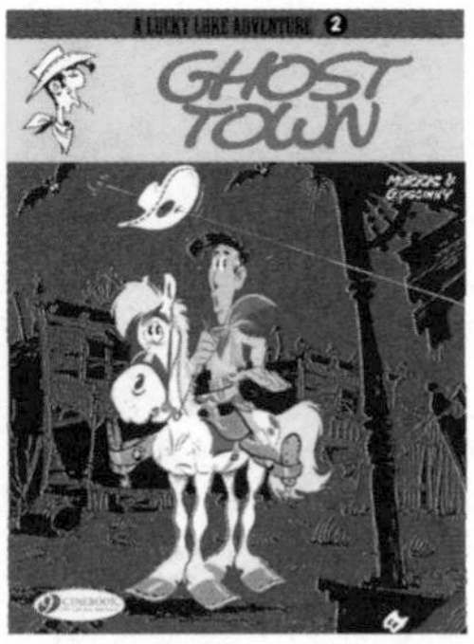
A LUCKY LUKE ADVENTURE 2
GHOST TOWN
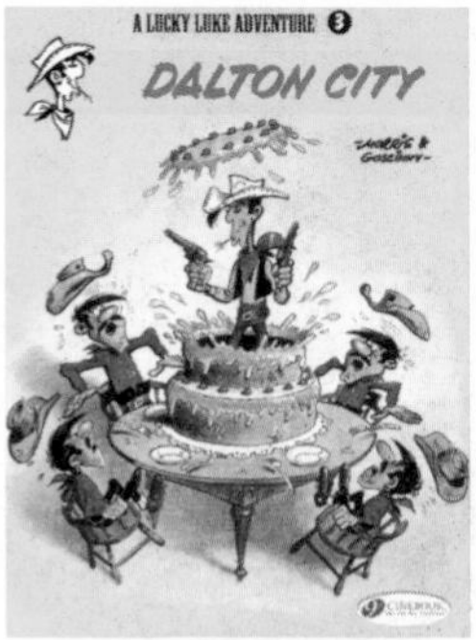
A LUCKY LUKE ADVENTURE 3
DALTON CITY
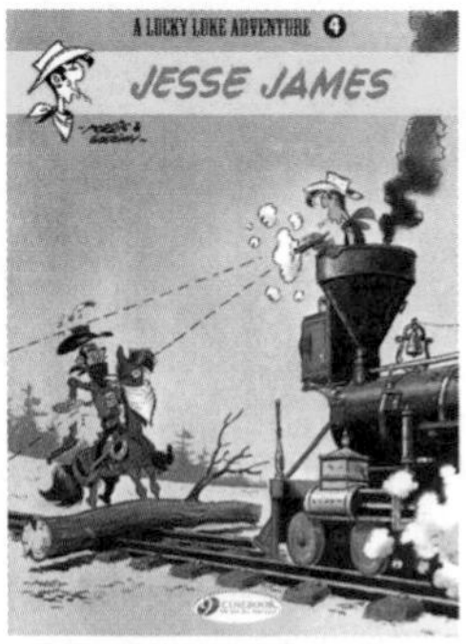
A LUCKY LUKE ADVENTURE 4
JESSE JAMES
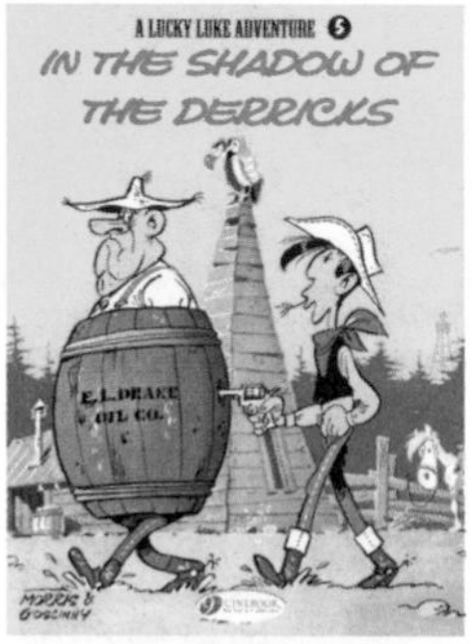
A LUCKY LUKE ADVENTURE 5
IN THE SHADOW OF THE DERRICKS
E. L. DRAKE OIL CO.
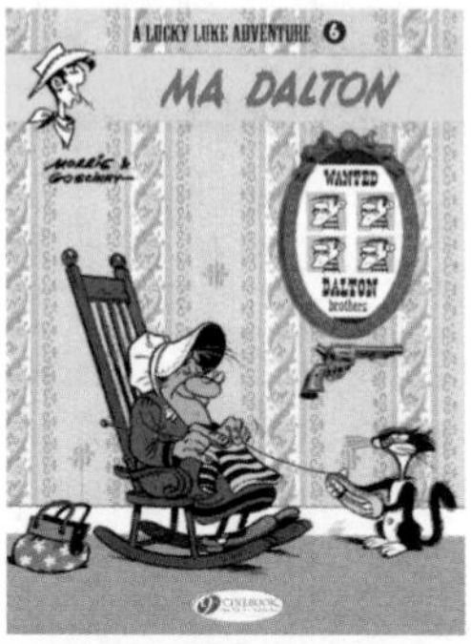
A LUCKY LUKE ADVENTURE 6
MA DALTON
WANTED
DALTON brothers
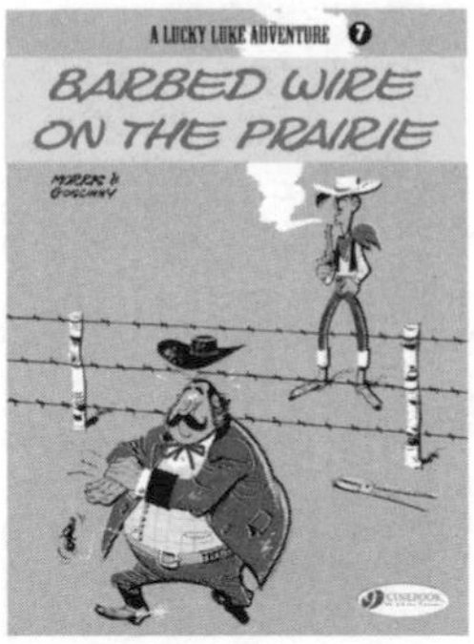
A LUCKY LUKE ADVENTURE 7
BARBED WIRE ON THE PRAIRIE
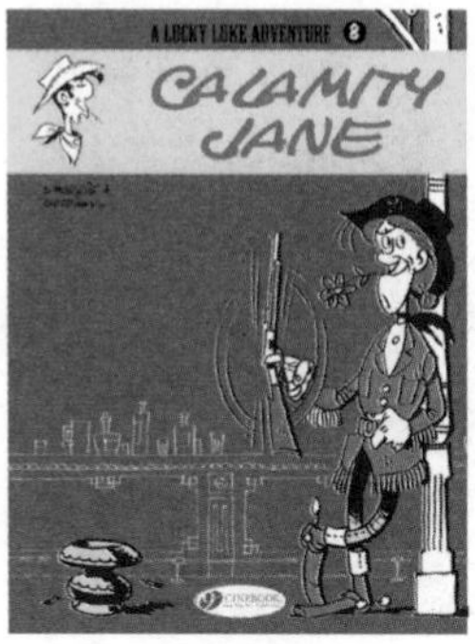
A LUCKY LUKE ADVENTURE 8
CALAMITY JANE
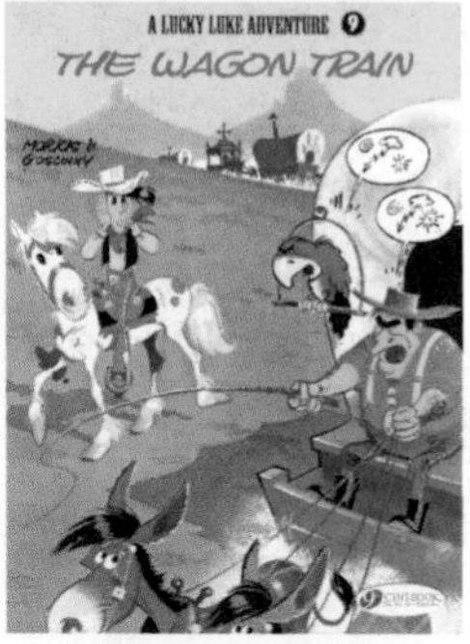
A LUCKY LUKE ADVENTURE 9
THE WAGON TRAIN
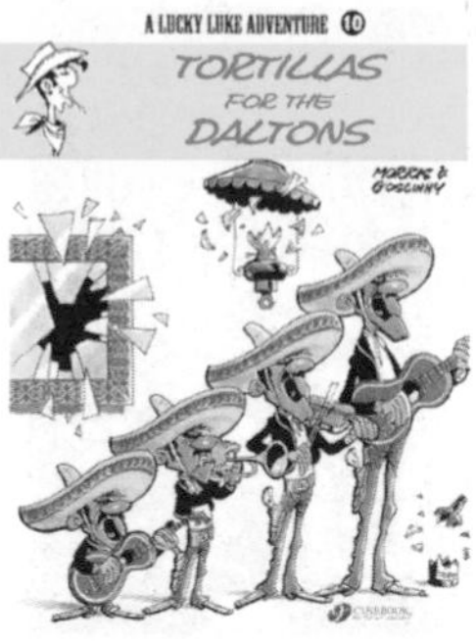
A LUCKY LUKE ADVENTURE 10
TORTILLAS FOR THE DALTONS
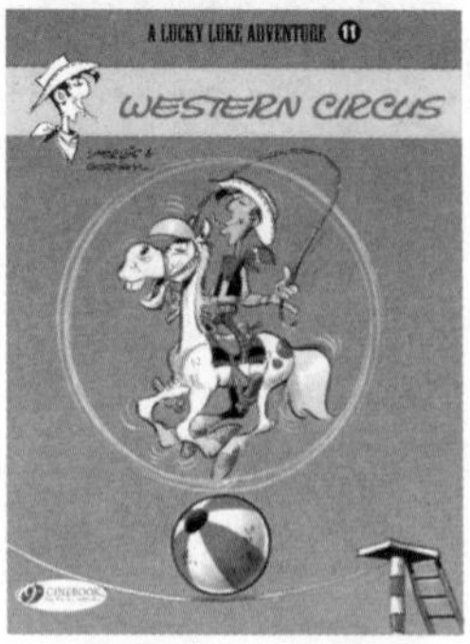
A LUCKY LUKE ADVENTURE 11
WESTERN CIRCUS
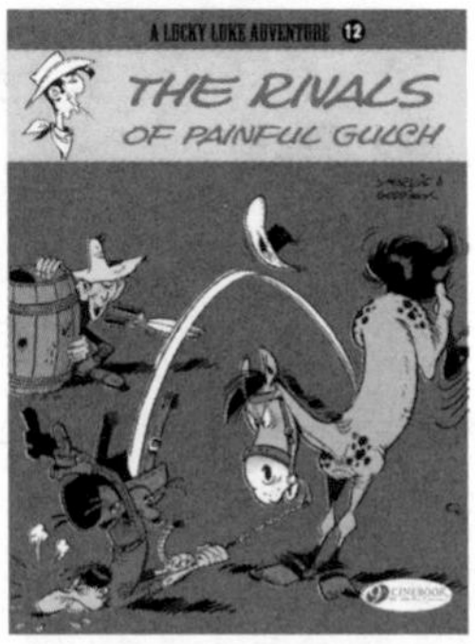
A LUCKY LUKE ADVENTURE 12
THE RIVALS OF PAINFUL GULCH
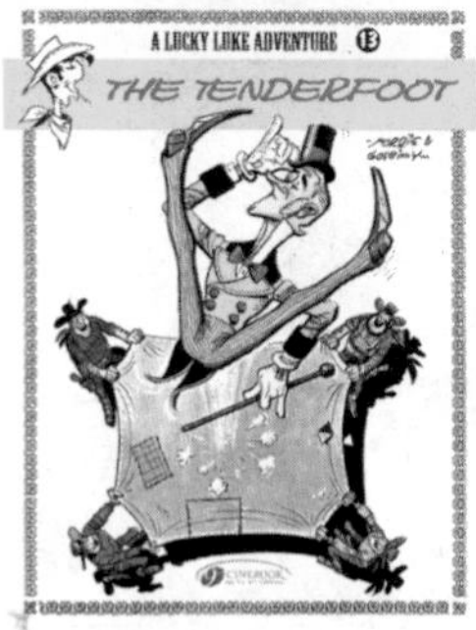
A LUCKY LUKE ADVENTURE 13
THE TENDERFOOT
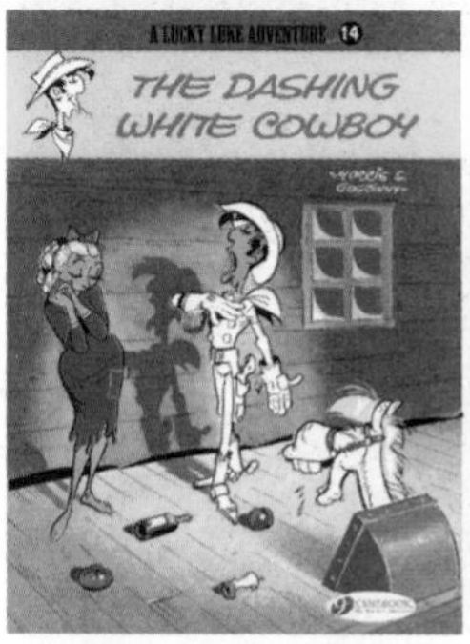
A LUCKY LUKE ADVENTURE 14
THE DASHING WHITE COWBOY
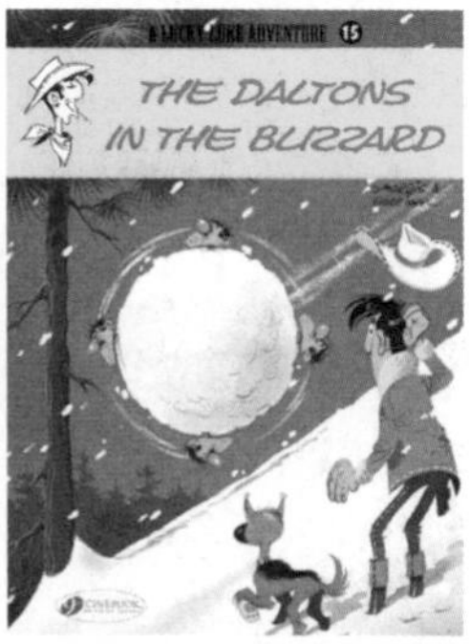
A LUCKY LUKE ADVENTURE 15
THE DALTONS IN THE BLIZZARD
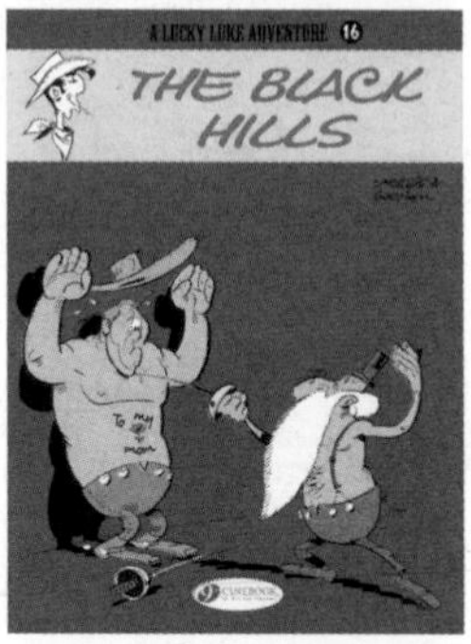
A LUCKY LUKE ADVENTURE 16
THE BLACK HILLS
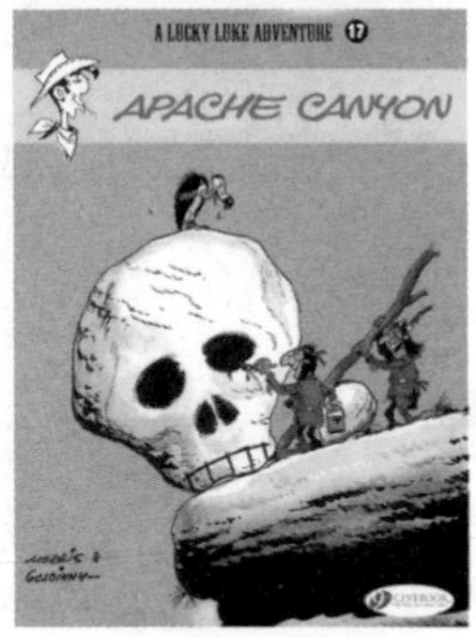
A LUCKY LUKE ADVENTURE 17
APACHE CANYON
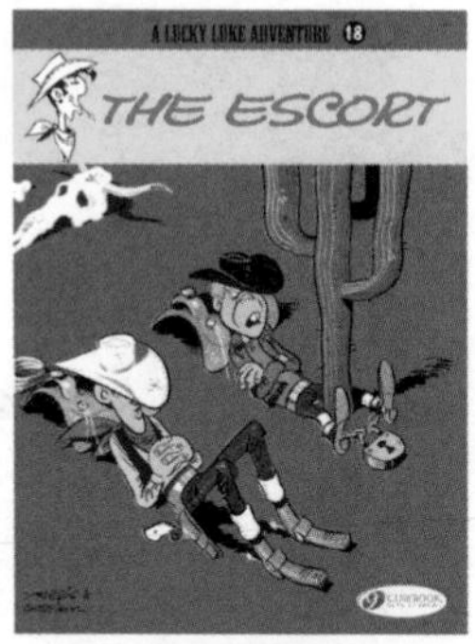
A LUCKY LUKE ADVENTURE 18
THE ESCORT
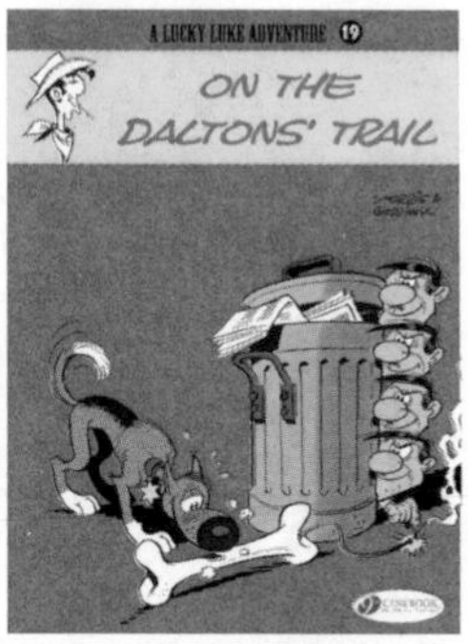
A LUCKY LUKE ADVENTURE 19
ON THE DALTONS' TRAIL
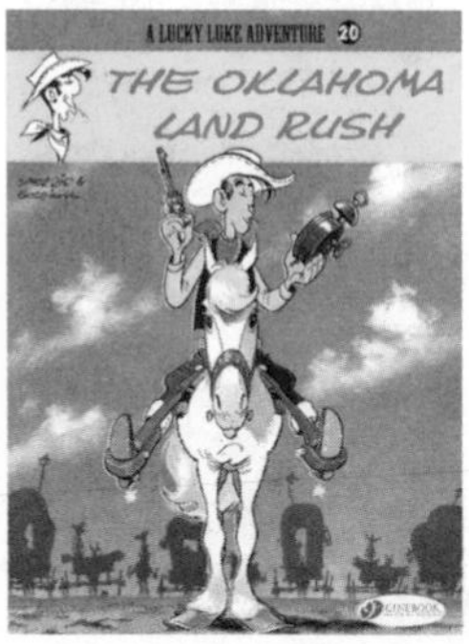
A LUCKY LUKE ADVENTURE 20
THE OKLAHOMA LAND RUSH
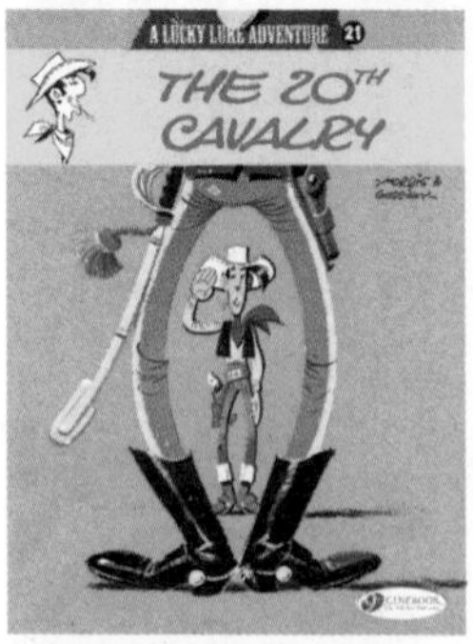
A LUCKY LUKE ADVENTURE 21
THE 20TH CAVALRY
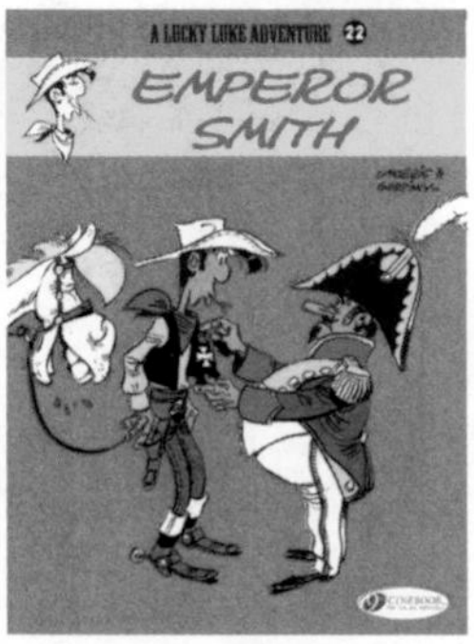
A LUCKY LUKE ADVENTURE 22
EMPEROR SMITH
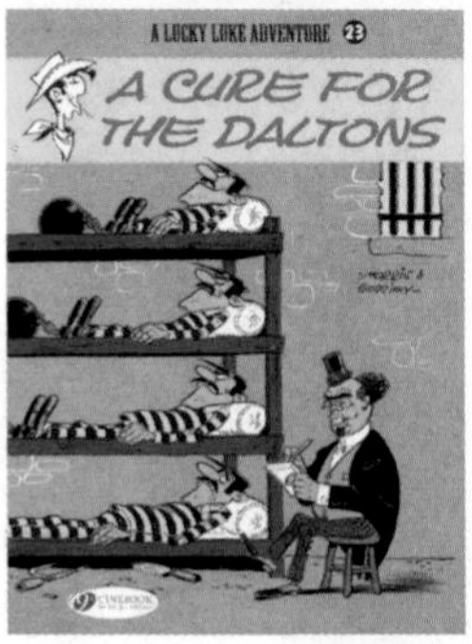
A LUCKY LUKE ADVENTURE 23
A CURE FOR THE DALTONS
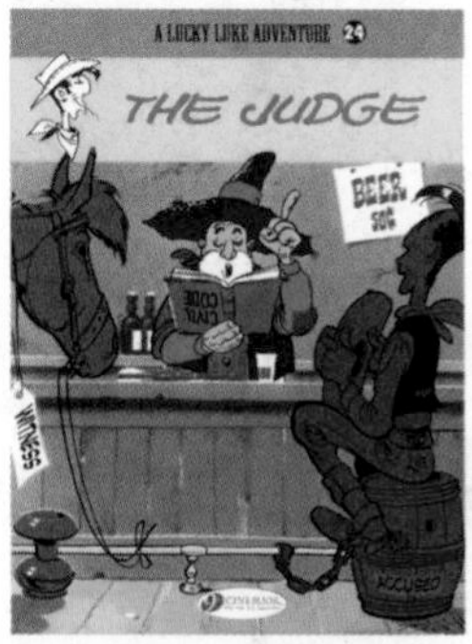
A LUCKY LUKE ADVENTURE 24
THE JUDGE
BEER
ACCUSED
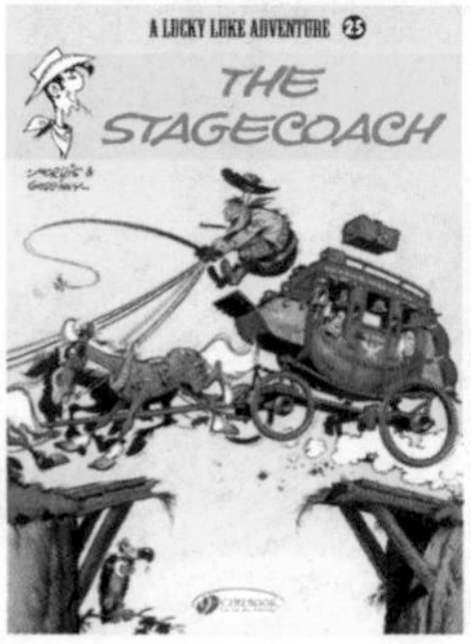
A LUCKY LUKE ADVENTURE 25
THE STAGECOACH
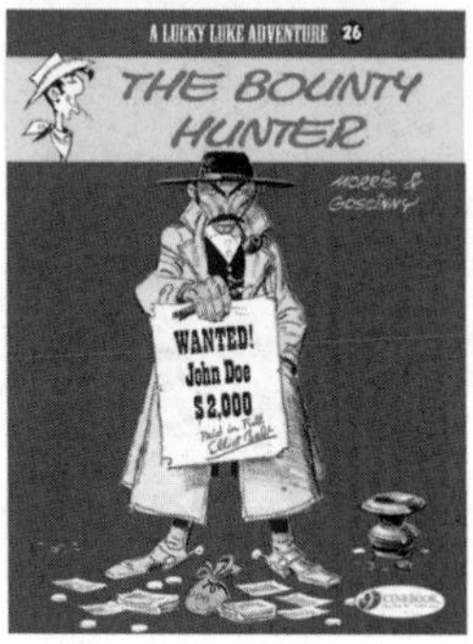
A LUCKY LUKE ADVENTURE 26
THE BOUNTY HUNTER
WANTED!
John Doe
$2,000
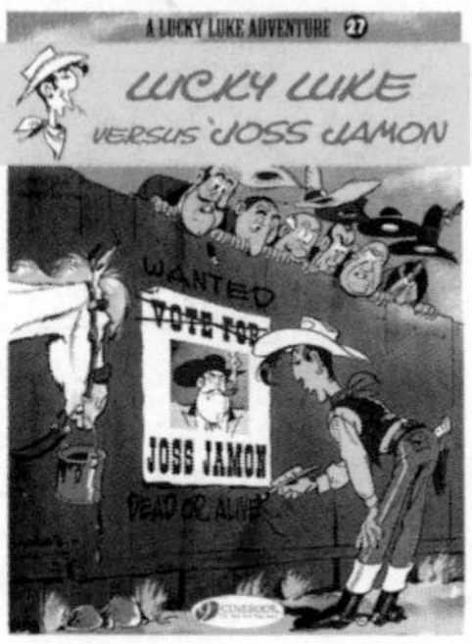
A LUCKY LUKE ADVENTURE 27
LUCKY LUKE VERSUS JOSS JAMON
WANTED
VOTE FOR
JOSS JAMON
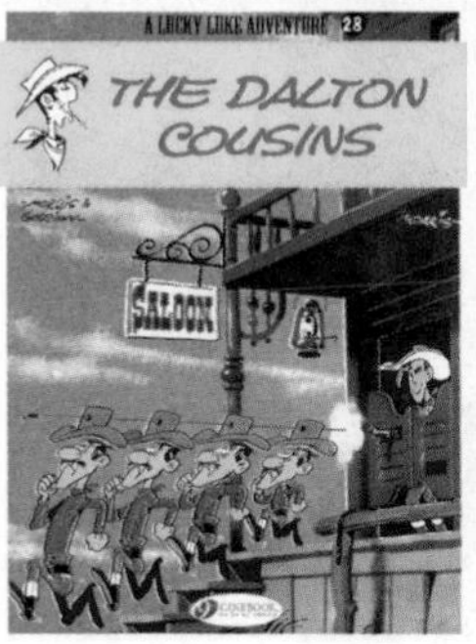
A LUCKY LUKE ADVENTURE 28
THE DALTON COUSINS
SALOON
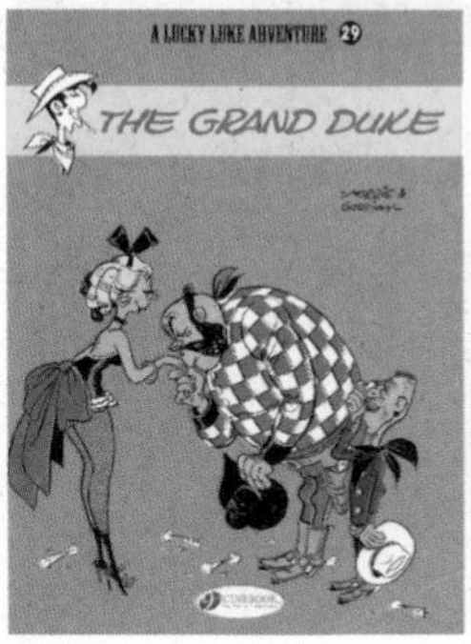
A LUCKY LUKE ADVENTURE 29
THE GRAND DUKE
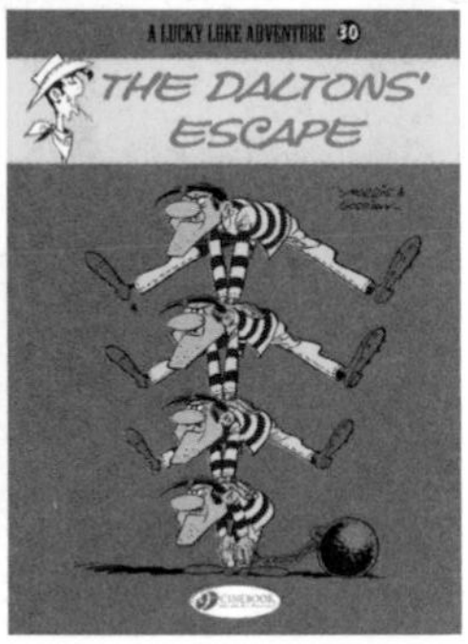
A LUCKY LUKE ADVENTURE 30
THE DALTONS' ESCAPE

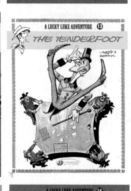

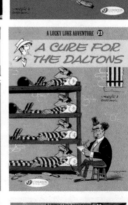

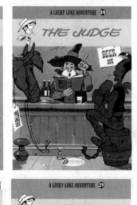

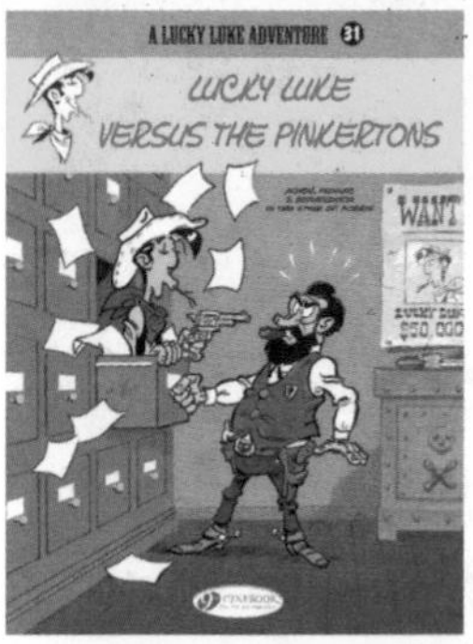
A LUCKY LUKE ADVENTURE 31
LUCKY LUKE VERSUS THE PINKERTONS
CINEBOOK

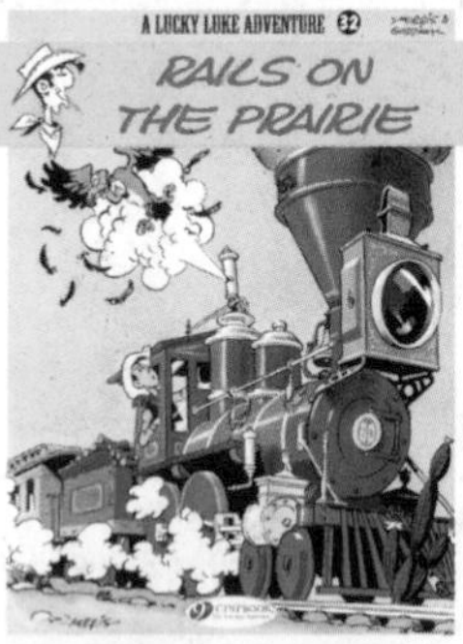
A LUCKY LUKE ADVENTURE 32
RAILS ON THE PRAIRIE
CINEBOOK

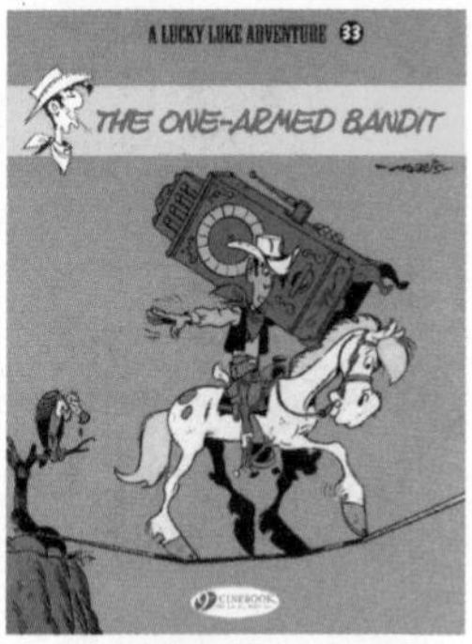
A LUCKY LUKE ADVENTURE 33
THE ONE-ARMED BANDIT
CINEBOOK

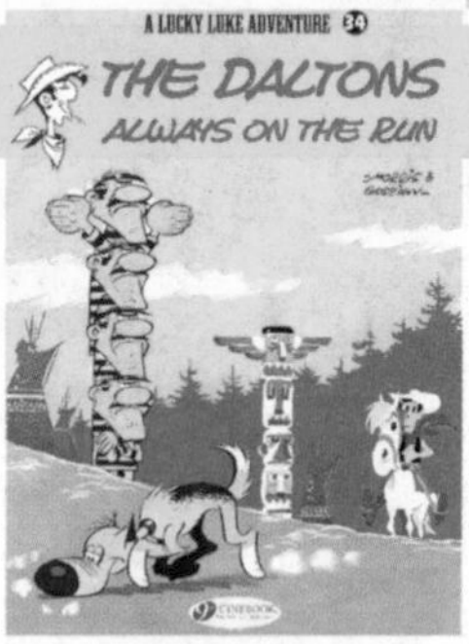
A LUCKY LUKE ADVENTURE 34
THE DALTONS ALWAYS ON THE RUN
CINEBOOK

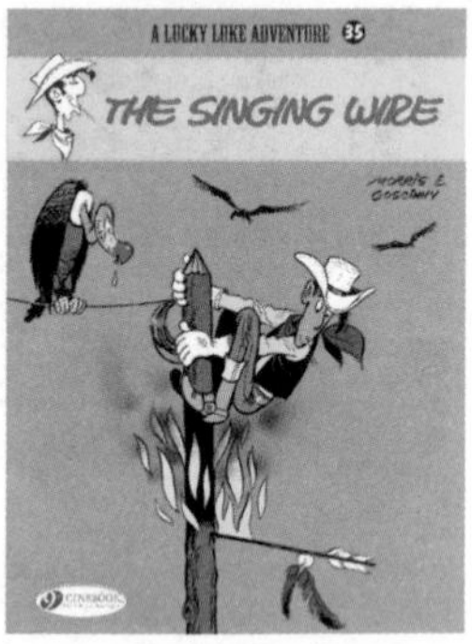
A LUCKY LUKE ADVENTURE 35
THE SINGING WIRE
CINEBOOK

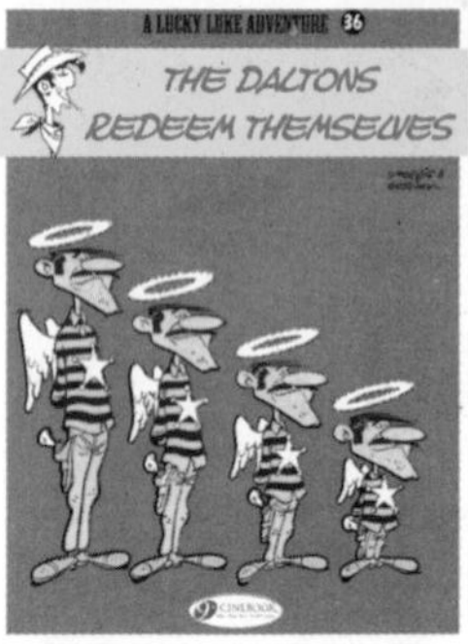
A LUCKY LUKE ADVENTURE 36
THE DALTONS REDEEM THEMSELVES
CINEBOOK

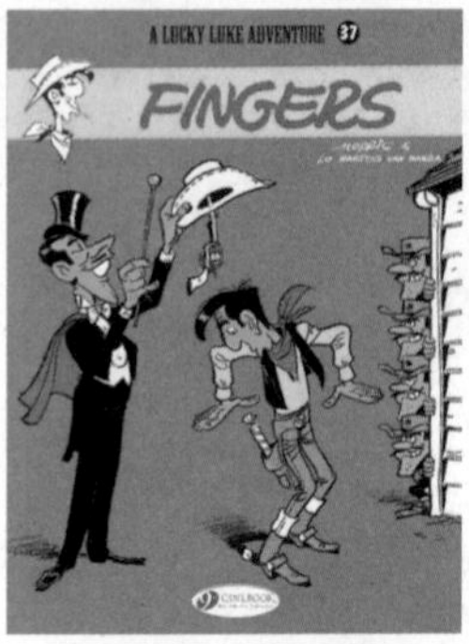
A LUCKY LUKE ADVENTURE 37
FINGERS
CINEBOOK

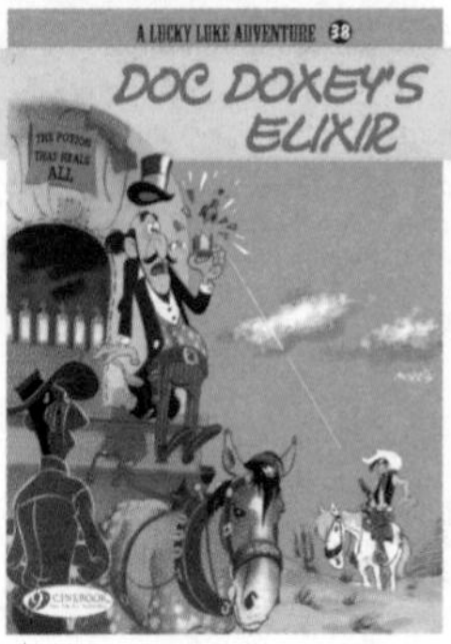
A LUCKY LUKE ADVENTURE 38
DOC DOXEY'S ELIXIR
CINEBOOK

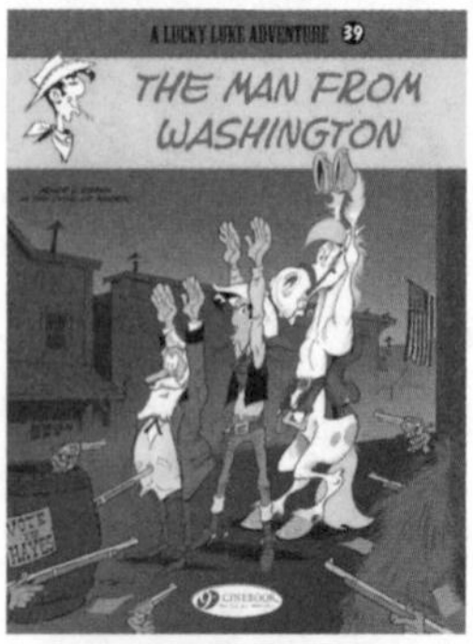
A LUCKY LUKE ADVENTURE 39
THE MAN FROM WASHINGTON
CINEBOOK

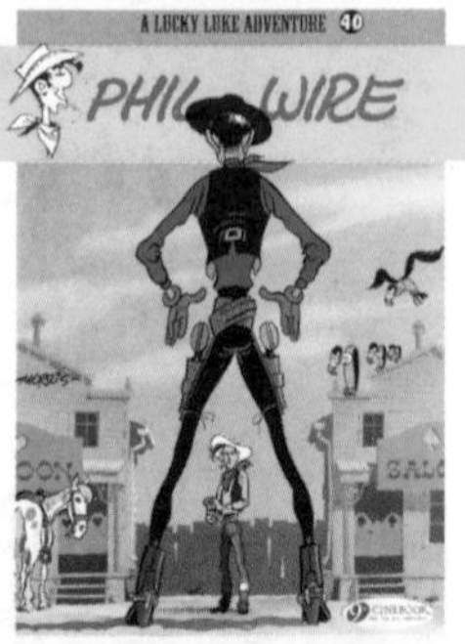
A LUCKY LUKE ADVENTURE 40
PHI WIRE
CINEBOOK

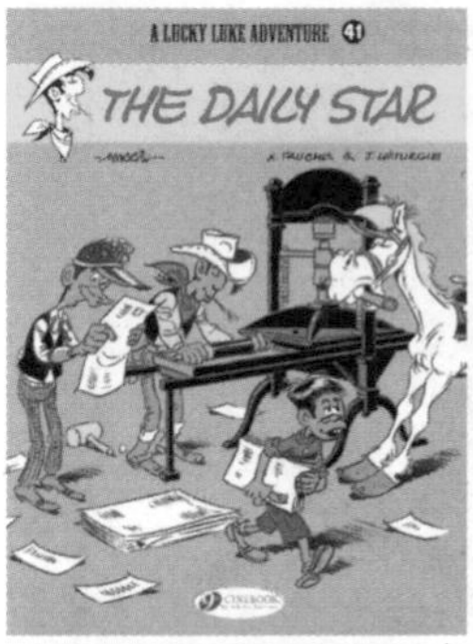
A LUCKY LUKE ADVENTURE 41
THE DAILY STAR
CINEBOOK

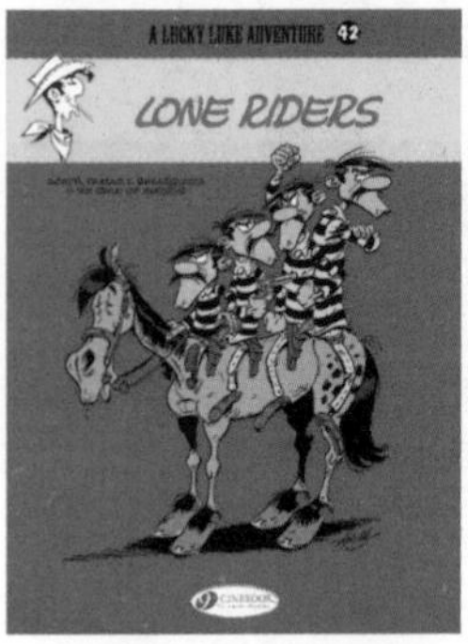
A LUCKY LUKE ADVENTURE 42
LONE RIDERS
CINEBOOK

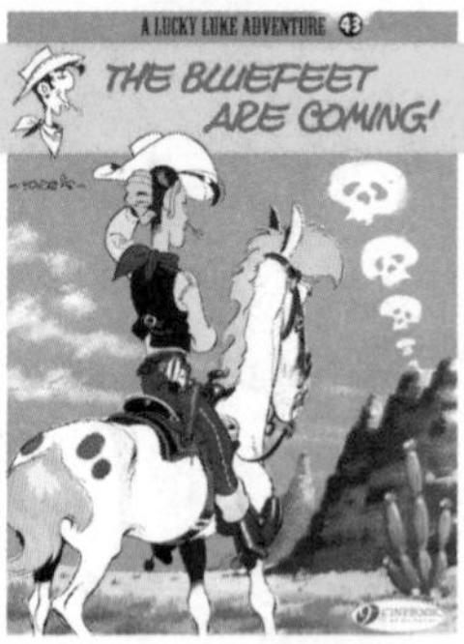
A LUCKY LUKE ADVENTURE 43
THE BLUEFEET ARE COMING!
CINEBOOK

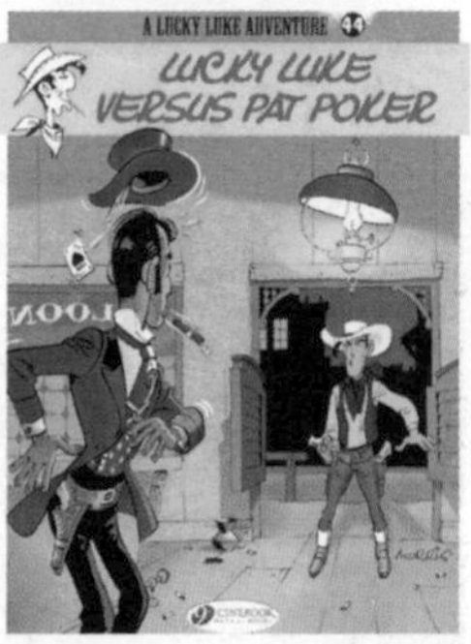
A LUCKY LUKE ADVENTURE 44
LUCKY LUKE VERSUS PAT POKER
CINEBOOK

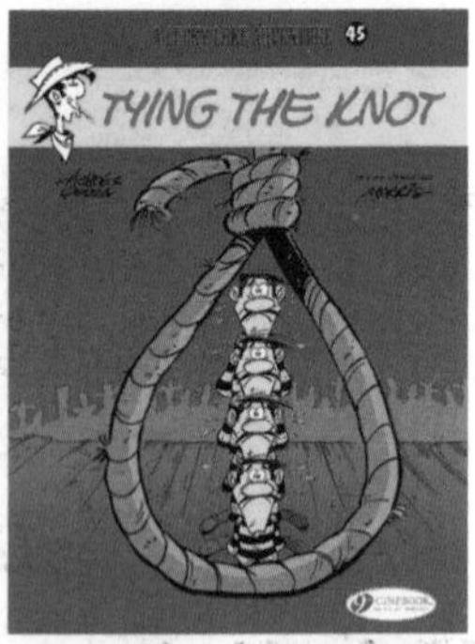
A LUCKY LUKE ADVENTURE 45
TYING THE KNOT
CINEBOOK

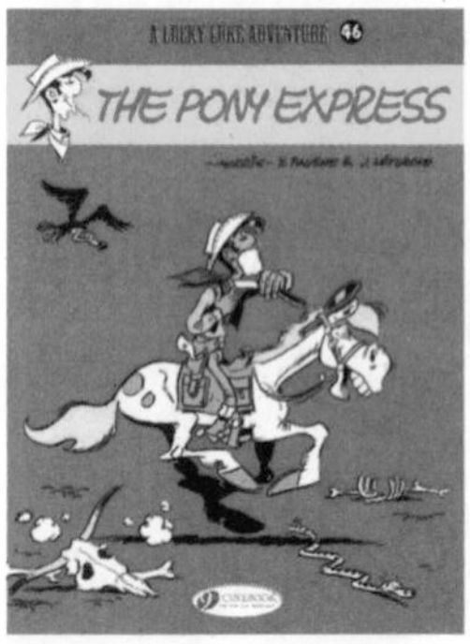
A LUCKY LUKE ADVENTURE 46
THE PONY EXPRESS
CINEBOOK

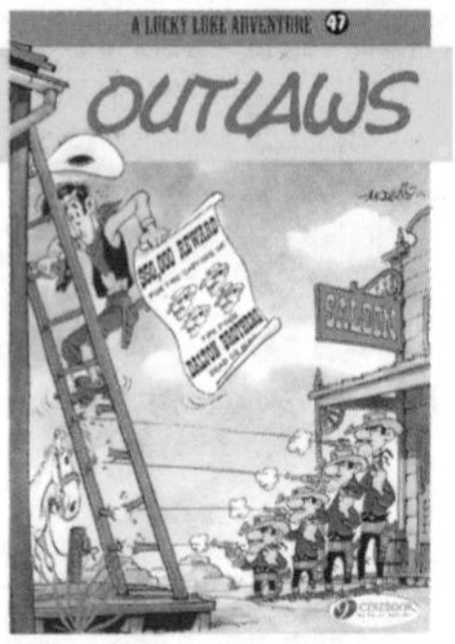
A LUCKY LUKE ADVENTURE 47
OUTLAWS
CINEBOOK

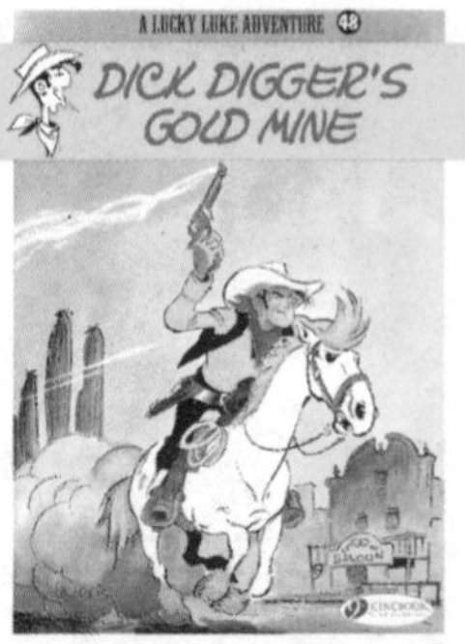
A LUCKY LUKE ADVENTURE 48
DICK DIGGER'S GOLD MINE
CINEBOOK

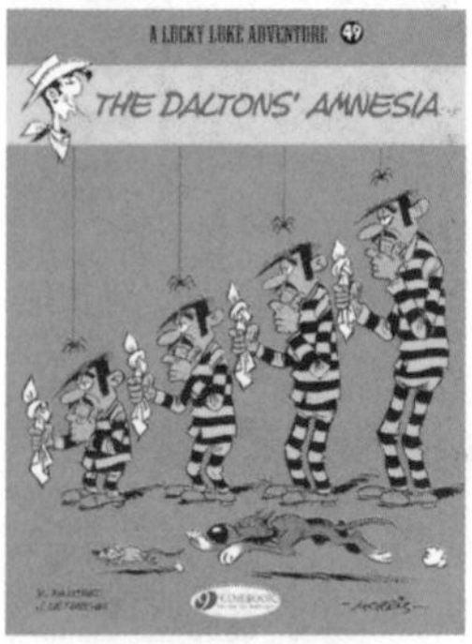
A LUCKY LUKE ADVENTURE 49
THE DALTONS' AMNESIA
CINEBOOK

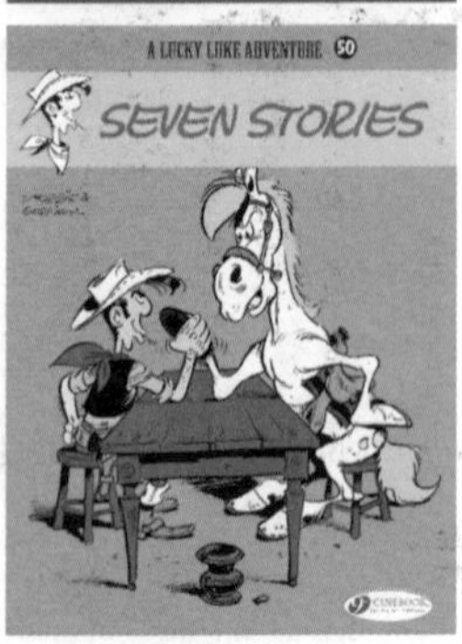
A LUCKY LUKE ADVENTURE 50
SEVEN STORIES
CINEBOOK

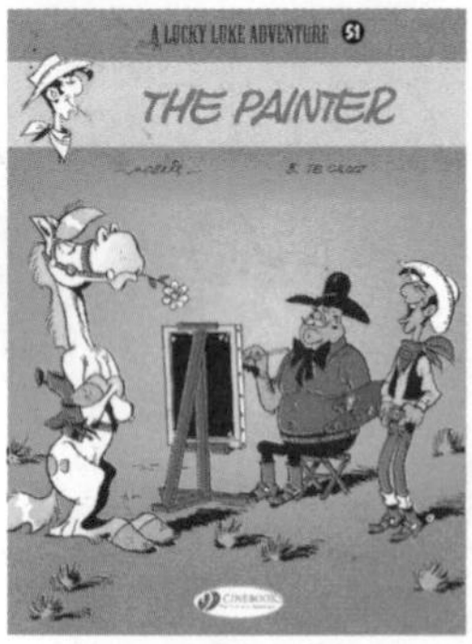
A LUCKY LUKE ADVENTURE 51
THE PAINTER
CINEBOOK

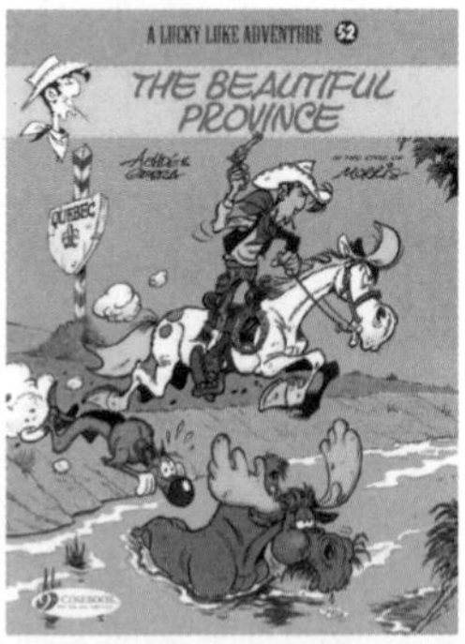
A LUCKY LUKE ADVENTURE 52
THE BEAUTIFUL PROVINCE
CINEBOOK

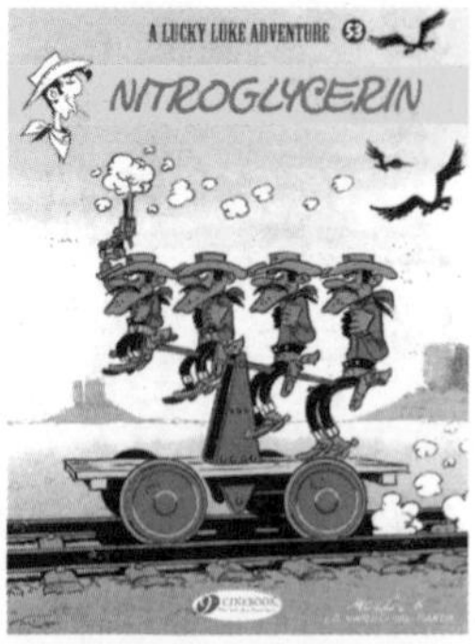
A LUCKY LUKE ADVENTURE 53
NITROGLYCERIN
CINEBOOK

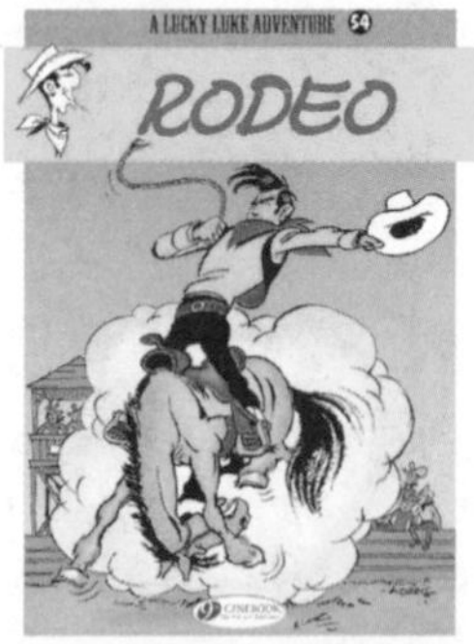
A LUCKY LUKE ADVENTURE 54
RODEO
CINEBOOK

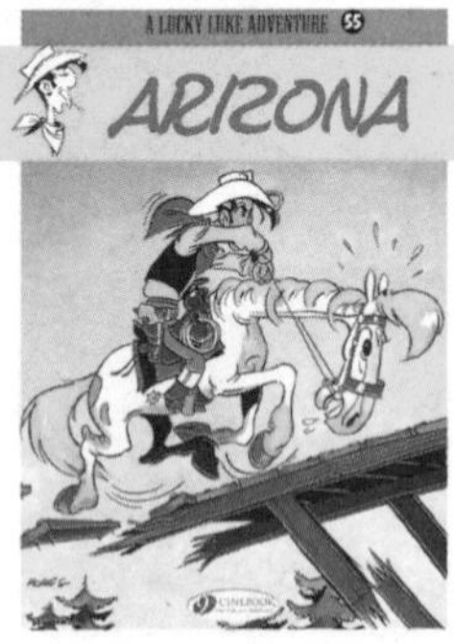
A LUCKY LUKE ADVENTURE 55
ARIZONA
CINEBOOK

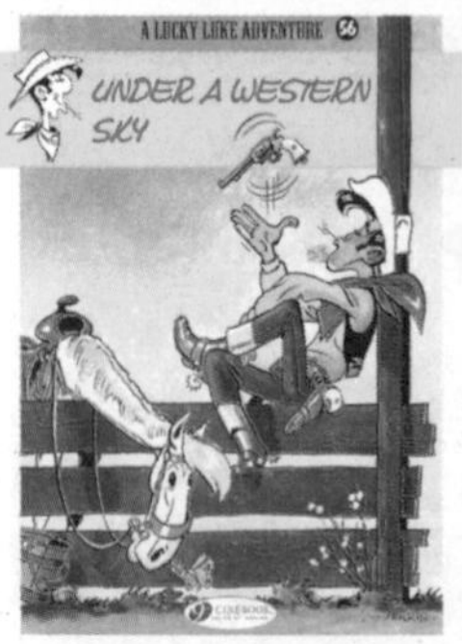
A LUCKY LUKE ADVENTURE 56
UNDER A WESTERN SKY
CINEBOOK

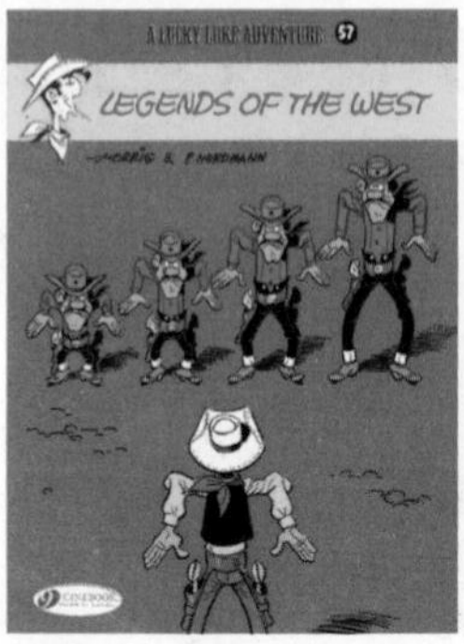
A LUCKY LUKE ADVENTURE 57
LEGENDS OF THE WEST
CINEBOOK

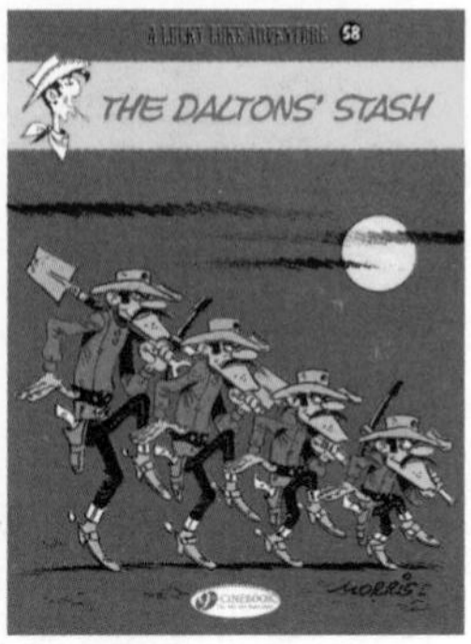
A LUCKY LUKE ADVENTURE 58
THE DALTONS' STASH
CINEBOOK

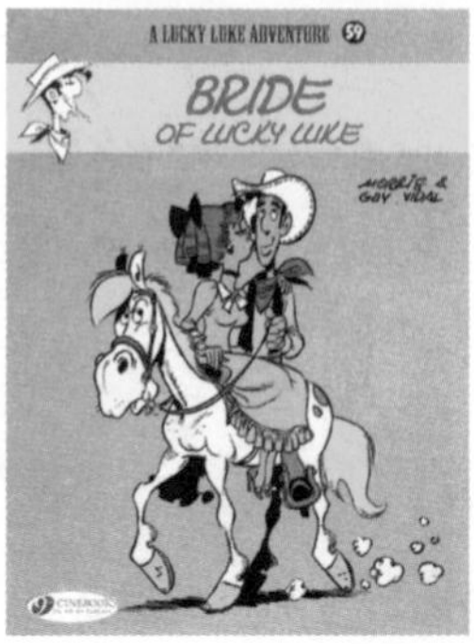
A LUCKY LUKE ADVENTURE 59
BRIDE OF LUCKY LUKE
CINEBOOK

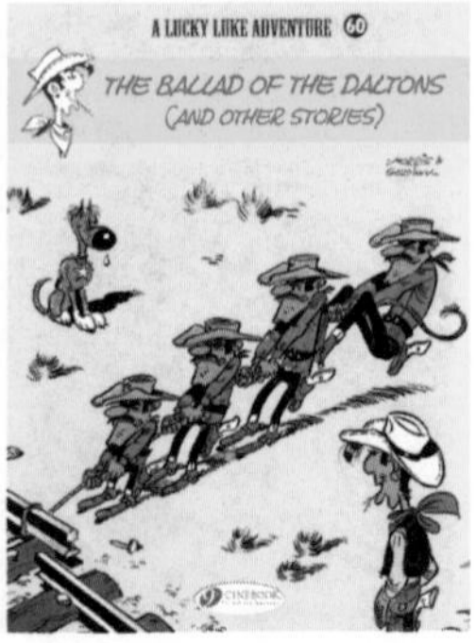
A LUCKY LUKE ADVENTURE 60
THE BALLAD OF THE DALTONS (AND OTHER STORIES)